2034

Book One: Sliding Doors

50-years after Orwell's dystopian nightmare, the world exists in a new nightmare

To Karen – for putting up with a shmuck like me for so many years

2034

1

July 4th, 2034

New York, New York

"Come on, come on – let's go!"

Noah Hodson struggled to put his sneakers on quickly. His mom stood by the open front door to their small apartment. "Mom, just a second!"

A minute later, the two of them sprinted out the front door of the building and began running across Third Avenue. A buzzing sound purred from Carol Hodson's purse.

They hit Lexington Avenue and Noah looked to his right. While no cars were visible up Lexington, he could see what looked like hundreds of people doing the same sprint as he and his mom.

His mom kept a tight grip on Noah's left hand. His small legs had trouble keeping up with her and she was simultaneously running and making sure that Noah did not fall behind.

The overhead speakers blared, "two minutes. The parade will begin in two minutes."

Noah looked up as they ran. Above his head was a large billboard of President Champer with a slight smile on his face. Below his face in large bold text was "Champer's First Rule". Noah began to read it, but the momentary distraction caused him to miss the curb as they hit Park Avenue and he fell to one knee. His mother also stumbled as a result. She quickly scooped him up in her arms, his knee was skinned, but she would worry about consoling him later.

They hit Madison Avenue when the one minute warning was given. Carol stopped to catch her breath, but she continued to hold Noah in her arms. He was sobbing from his bloody knee.

After taking ten seconds to catch her breath. Carol began the final run to Fifth Avenue. They arrived with seconds to spare and settled into the massive crowds that lined the sides of Fifth Avenue.

Noah stopped crying and instead was fascinated by the loud buzzing sound that now surrounded them. Although he was only nine years old, he soon realized that the buzzing was coming from not just his mother's cellphone, but everyone's cellphone.

A moment later the buzzing abruptly stopped. Noah looked over his mother's shoulder back in the direction they had come. He saw what looked to be a family of four or five running across Madison Avenue, a block from where the crowd had gathered.

A moment later, an army truck cut in front of the family. When the truck pulled away a minute later, the family was gone.

Noah turned away when he heard the rumbling sound coming down Fifth Avenue.

From his vantage point in his mother's arms, he could make out the tanks that were now rolling down the street.

His mom yelled into his ear above the loud roar of the tanks. "Honey, we need to cheer."

Noah dutifully began to yell in celebration. All around them, the people did the same. "USA, USA, USA!"

Carol put down her son as she needed a break. Although it was still early, the temperature was already above 80 degrees and the large crowd made it oppressively hot. Carol's shirt was soaked through from the combination of the run, the heat of the day and her son's body heat.

Noah used the opportunity of his new found freedom to make his way through the crowd to the edge of Fifth Avenue to get a better look.

All the way up Fifth, the military parade extended. In addition to the tanks that rolled by, Noah could see soldiers marching in column, machine guns on display, and jeeps loaded with various generals and other high ranking officials. Noah raised his hand in salute.

The overhead speakers began to play the National Anthem and everyone dutifully stopped cheering and put their hands over their hearts.

Carol Hodson had finally pushed her way through the crowd to recover her son. She put her hand on Noah's shoulder and leaned down to whisper in his ear. "Noah, honey, we need to sing. Just like we did it last night."

The crowd began to sing in unison. Noah did his best to sing along; although, he could not remember all of the words.

He looked across the street and saw a group of about ten men take a knee as one of the jeeps carrying the generals road by. The kneeling men held out their right fists, but otherwise did not appear to be hostile.

A moment later, the crowd on the west side of the street parted around the kneeling men and a squad of police swarmed them.

Noah continued to sing as he watched the men get dragged away from the street; although, they did not appear to put up much of a resistance to the police. A moment later, the crowd closed around where the men had just been. The singing continued.

2

June 27th, 2034

Los Angeles, California

Larry woke suddenly from what had been a fitful rest. The clock said 5:03, which meant he only had seven minutes until the unwavering blaring would begin. Rather than catch the last few minutes of sleep, Larry deftly rolled to the side of the bed, the cold feel of the tile on his bare feet helping to push him to wakefulness, and slowly twisted his back from side-to-side, making sure that his sudden movements would not awaken old injuries.

The sounds from his window threatened the usual 5 AM rigors. The curfew that had begun the week before following what had quickly been dubbed "the Santa Monica massacre" was still in effect and Larry could hear the distant cry of the Ajax 400 speakers that warned anyone who ventured outside could be "shot on site".

It was funny what one got used to. In another life, one left behind almost 10-years before, Larry would have struggled to sleep through even the slightest disturbance. But now, the incessant blaring of what amounted to death threats were not enough to keep him from catching four hours of shuteye.

Larry stood to get a closer look at the street below. While he had grown-up resenting rubberneckers, who insisted on slowing his commute, he now admitted to himself that checking the streets for someone who might have ventured out during the on-again/off-again curfew and caught an unfortunate government bullet was one of his favorite pastimes, regardless of how much it sickened him to think that this was the world he now lived in.

Alas, the streets were empty (he had yet to actually see a body, but morbidly, there was always hope) and Larry made the short trudge to the bathroom.

On the way, he reflexively looked at the other side of the bed. She wasn't coming back and Larry knew it – a volley of bullets had seen to that. But every day for the last eleven-years he still looked. Her side of the bed undisturbed. Never slept in by Larry, nor anyone else for that matter.

The bathroom light interrupted Larry's brief foray with the past. He squinted and stared at the fuzzy visage in the mirror. The muscular tone that he had been so proud of when Beth and Jack and the Spooner had still been a part of his life had given way to pockets of softness. He was still fit, largely because there was never quite enough to eat and work put a lot of stress on his muscles, but he was far from "my well-toned killing machine" as Beth had once affectionately called him in her weird way.

Resigned to his softness, Larry began to brush his teeth. He hated the taste of it in his mouth, and briefly longed for some Crest or any minted brand name as opposed to the tasteless rations he now subsisted on.

Larry spit out the mostly tasteless paste and did his usual quick facial check. Despite the passage of time, Larry still worried that the scars would be visible to someone who studied his face. He slowly turned his head to the left and to the right, running his fingers over the area just to the outside of each of his deep blue eyes. Satisfied that the only lines were those that reflected his age, Larry wiped his hands.

Pat...pat...pat

Larry looked up at the mirror and then at the bathroom door.

Pat...pat...pat...pat and then distant yells.

Larry instinctively moved to the bedroom and crouched as he approached the window. Someone had fired a gun, a sound that Larry would recognize no matter how far away it was discharged and he was going to get a look.

Pat..pat

Closer to the window, Larry put the shots at less than a block away from his apartment. From his view three floors up, he couldn't see anything on the street below, but whoever was shooting, was close by. Larry scanned the outside from a crouched position just above the window sill and then pivoted back to the bed, instinctively reaching under the right corner of the bedspring.

He drew his Glock from its hidden location and pivoted back to the window. Larry felt better with the Glock in his hand. Although he oiled and cleaned it regularly, this was the first time in years he could remember holding it for comfort and he admitted to himself as he scanned the street below that it felt good. An old appendage awakened following years of neglect.

Footsteps – running hard.

A shape rounded the corner and sprinted across the street just under Larry's window. Larry couldn't tell from his position, but he suspected it was a woman by the size of the figure and the way that she ran. Athletic to be sure, but something supine about the gait.

At the same time Larry heard the downstairs door of his building kicked open, three other figures rounded the corner.

Pat...pat...pat...pat...pat

Five semi-silenced rounds ricocheted off of Larry's building. These guys were good as the bullets had come fast and generally right at where the fleeing figure had been only moments before.

Larry reflexively chambered a round and moved toward the door to his one room apartment. Whoever was fleeing would be outside his door in seconds. Larry knelt and listened as footsteps moved closer to his door. He silently wished that they would pass, but then Larry heard a soft tapping on the door. He knelt there – frozen.

A voice from the other side of the door whispered, "please, I need help." Larry was now certain it was a woman.

Larry pointed the gun at the door. He aimed down the barrel and then lowered the gun. "Fuck," he silently muttered to himself.

Whoever was chasing the girl would be on the building in seconds. It was time to decide.

Larry had not given a shit in nearly a decade, but something about the last sixty seconds had awoken something in him. He shuffled to the door, keeping low and as he reached for the door knob with his left hand, he pointed the gun once again with his right.

He then opened the door and a woman pushed her way in and Larry quickly and quietly shut the door behind her.

Larry turned to the woman and found himself staring down the barrel of what appeared to be a .38. Fuck, he was rusty. The woman motioned with the gun and Larry nodded. He put down his own gun and moved silently to the foot of his bed. The woman sat next to him, still pointing the gun at him. She had short blond hair and a strikingly beautiful face. Despite her efforts in evading the men outside, she looked both calm and un-winded.

They now heard the three pursuers come crashing in from below and then footsteps flying up the steps.

"Can I lower this?"

Larry nodded. The woman stared at him for two beats and then lowered the weapon. They then heard footsteps go flying by the other side of the door.

"They are going to go to the top and then door to door on the way down. One of them is waiting downstairs. I'm Karen." She said this in a low whisper while staring at Larry and without pausing.

Larry nodded silently. While her description of what they would do was remarkably detailed –

Larry did not doubt that this was "regular government procedure".

Larry whispered, "what's the play?"

Karen stared at Larry and his use of the phrase. "Either I or we go down, take out the guy they left by the door and get the hell out of here."

Larry nodded. He looked at the door and then back at the woman. For the second time in the past few minutes, he had to decide whether he wanted to go back to his old life or continue to embrace the new one. He paused for a second and then decided, "we", he mouthed and then pointed at his gun, which was lying near the door. Karen smiled and nodded and then turned to look at the weapon and then back at Larry. She nodded again.

Larry moved silently to the gun. He then looked back at Karen as he moved to the door. She then said, "wait. We need something quieter – no guns."

Larry looked at her and seemed to contemplate her statement for a moment. He then nodded and held up a finger and pointed to the closet. Karen nodded back.

Larry then moved quickly to the closet and reached inside the door, drawing his well warn 2018 Louisville Slugger, which had been a second birthday gift for the Spooner when the world had still been a "normal place". He began to tuck his Glock into his pajama pants and at that moment realized that he was still wearing his pajama pants.

Yesterday's pair of jeans sat in the corner and despite his new company, Larry silently ripped off his pajama pants and threw on the jeans and then slipped on his runners – socks would have to wait.

Larry looked at Karen and said, "I'll take point." She nodded and attempted not to betray any reaction to his use of "point". Larry then opened the door and gave a quick glance up the stairs. Satisfied, he turned back to Karen and nodded.

They moved to the third floor landing and Larry held up one finger. He then knelt by his door and leaned the bat against the wall. He then removed a small plate from the base of the wall and worked on something that Karen could not see. After about ten seconds, Larry grabbed the bat and then rose back to his full height of roughly six feet and nodded to Karen. She stared back at him briefly not entirely sure of what he had just done.

Larry and Karen moved quickly, but silently down the stairs. As they rounded the corner on the second floor, Larry motioned to Karen to stop. He made his way to the far side of the stairs, which were blanketed in darkness – the first time Larry had silently thanked the government for rationing all nature of things.

Larry crept down the stairs and saw the man stationed by the door bathed in the light of the street. He was big, but unprofessional. Standing as he was, he had blocked the door, but he had no view of what was coming down the stairs as the positioning of the light behind him prevented much of a view inside.

Larry could have shot him without risk, but as Karen had noted, escape depended on the two other pursuers taking their time in making it back to street level.

At the base of the stairs, Larry knew he would have to take the last five feet or so in view of his victim. It had been a number of years, but a strange calmness settled on Larry as he devised and executed his plan.

He hit the landing and in four quick strides cut the distance to four feet. The doorman heard Larry before he saw him and raised his pistol. At the same time, Larry dropped into a slide and swung the bat through the doorman's right knee. The sound of breaking bone pleased Larry as the doorman grunted in pain, firing one partially silenced shot into the ceiling as he toppled backwards to the ground.

Larry fluidly rolled to his knees and with two hands swung the bat down on the doorman's face, probably breaking multiple bones in the process. The man grunted and appeared to be unconscious. Larry rose whispering for Karen to come down.

Larry stood there for a moment and then realized that he was no longer holding the whole bat. The bat had split in half and he was left just holding about 12-inches of the handle. He stared down at the handle with both a sense of satisfaction and sadness. The Spooner's second birthday – the image of a rainbow briefly popped into Larry's head.

Karen arrived at the door to the building looking at Larry's handiwork with a sense of deep respect. The two of them moved the doorman inside the door and into the shadows, Karen picked up his gun. Karen put her gun in her pocket, preferring the silenced weapon and the two of them prepared to move outside. As they were about the exit, Karen whispered, "wait" and held Larry's arm. She looked at her watch and after about ten-seconds nodded.

The two left the building being sure to keep pressed to Larry's side of the street until they rounded the corner where they paused in the darkness.

"I'm Larry."

3

July 17th, 1987

Moscow, Soviet Union

Richard Champer stepped off the plane and was greeted by Russian Ambassador to the United States Yuri Chesnakoff and two other men that Champer did not know.

"The flight was good, no?" Yuri smiled as he asked him in his thick Russian accent.

Champer nodded and winked. "A beautiful flight, Yuri, just beautiful."

Yuri introduced the two other men to Champer. One was a high level attaché in the Soviet government, while the other was Yuri's new aide. Champer had trouble understanding their last names, but understood that one was Pavel and the younger one was Dimitri.

They drove in a stretch Lincoln to the National Hotel in downtown Moscow. "You will be staying in the Lenin Suite, it is very nice." Yuri was pleased with himself.

Champer looked out the window as the Moscow landscape zoomed by. He smiled. "Yuri, I get the feeling this is going to be a long and fruitful relationship."

4

July 6th, 2023

Sacramento, California

Governor George Beachum stared at his top aide.

"Bill, I'm doing this."

William "Big Bill" Tanner stared back at the man he had grown to love over the past 22-years, his mouth slightly agape, sweat beginning to form in his pits. "Okay, but George, can we talk about it?"

Beachum smiled, "talk – yes, talk me out of it – no. We have bent and we've bent and still they fuck us over and over again," he said the last part while briefly searching the air for the right words before settling on something a bit cruder than he had intended.

Tanner nodded, "Okay, I get that – they don't play by the same set of rules as we do. But what you are suggesting is basically taking the fuckin' rule book, dropping a nuke on it and then crapping on the remains for good measure."

Beachum smiled. Tanner had always been a "one-upper" when it came to levels of crude and he hadn't disappointed. "I'm sick of incrementalism, Bill. Not to be too dramatic, but every time we step an inch, they step a yard and ultimately it doesn't end up as tit for tat, but tit for rat-a-tat-tat."

Tanner now shared a smile, "Ironical you making it about tits when we are talking about the tit-grabber."

Beachum smiled more broadly, "not my intention, but I agree it fits." Beachum then paused and his smile slowly faded, "Look Bill, they have stepped on everything we believe in, over and over again and we have largely taken it. They ripped families apart at the border and we took it. They turned ICE into some version of the Gestapo and we took it. They shredded every piece of environmental legislation we championed and we took it. They took every ounce of civility this country held dear and we took it. But taking away a woman's right to choose when that's who got me fuckin elected? I'm not going to take that and frankly, Billy, I shouldn't have taken any of the other atrocities that came before it."

Tanner stared at him for a beat. "Okay, walk me through how you think this plays out."

Beachum smiled again. "I thought that's why I paid you the big bucks."

Tanner smiled back and after a brief pause. "Well, I think you just announce it. I'm not sure [hesitating]. Actually, I'm pretty sure that there is no right way to do this because frankly this country was set up on the principal that you would never have to do this."

Beachum stared back at Tanner for several seconds. "You know what pisses me off more than all the rest, Bill? That fucker calling me Boring Beachum. It's not even fucking clever, it's something a fifth grader would come up with – not the fucking President of this great country. At least spend 10 minutes coming up with something better than Boring fuckin' Beachum."

"ImPeachum."

Beachum laughed. "That's what I mean – how long did that take you? Eight fuckin' seconds and Big Bill Tanner, who can barely spell just out-clevered the leader of the free fuckin' world." Chortling, "Impeachum, that's pretty fuckin' good."

Tanner laughed quietly. "Not to be ironical again, George, but when you stride up to the podium and announce that California is beginning the process of seceding from the Union, the moronic fifth grader might just come up with ImPeachum on his own."

5

June 27th, 2034

Los Angeles, California

"Why'd you help me, Larry?"

Larry stared back at Karen. They were in a copse of trees in Klein Park, watching the sun slowly rise. "Not sure I really know why. Just seemed like the thing to do at the time."

Karen stared back at him, studying his face through the dim light. She decided quickly that something was slightly off about his look – the eyes didn't quite match the face. He was good looking to be sure, despite the fact he looked to have at least 15-years on her, but something wasn't quite right. "That's a pretty big "right thing to do", Larry. Do you often take a baseball bat to a man's head for women you don't know?"

Larry sat down against a tree and stared up at Karen. "I'm not sure I really thought about it. But when you put it that way – no, I cannot recall taking a bat to someone's head for a woman I just met. At least recently."

Karen gave a skeptical laugh and continued to stand over Larry. "Who the fuck are you?"

"What do you mean?"

"I mean that your takeout of the guy at the door was nothing short of a work of art. Regular guys who have just woken up from a deep sleep and then randomly taken in a damsel in distress don't pull off professional hits against a professional the way you just did – even on their best days."

"Why were those men chasing you?"

She smiled. "I was out after curfew."

Larry shook his head. "Bullshit, those guys weren't gestapo, they were trained killers, who were pursuing a person of interest, which by the looks of it – was you."

Karen curled her lip in a half-smile at Larry's use of "gestapo". "I'm going to trust you with something, Larry."

Larry stood up. "I have to get to work."

Karen gave another skeptical laugh. "You can't go to work, Larry. Those other two idiots are going to go door to door on their way down and they are going to find your apartment empty. They are then going to find the doorman with his head bashed in. It is not going to take long for you to become a person of interest in this whole thing."

Larry brushed the dirt from the back of his jeans. "I'll be fine."

Karen smiled. "Who the fuck are you?"

Larry squinted and then stared at Karen. "Just a guy who did an impulsive thing and helped a damsel in distress." He turned to look at the rising sun. "I have to go."

"Where will you go back to? I mean, okay, you go to work and then what? Your apartment is compromised, so you can't go back there after work. Then what?"

Larry had to admit that he had not thought that through. His fingers hurt from swinging the bat and again he thought about the Spooner. Had it really been more than ten-years? "I'll figure it out." Larry started to walk away and Karen put her hand on his shoulder. He shuddered silently – how long had it been?

"Okay, go. But come to 14 Wesson after work. I owe you. Probably more than I can ever repay, but at least I can give you a place to go tonight."

Larry turned and stared back at Karen. He looked down at her hand and then back at her face. "Let me think about it, but thanks."

The "but thanks" seemed to tell her that he was unlikely to take her up on her offer. Karen watched him walk away. He moved toward a garbage can and made a quick move to the base before resuming his walk. Had she not been staring at him, she might have missed the quick move, which she figured was designed to hide the gun. "You are good, Larry."

6

July 7th, 2023

Sacramento, California

"I want to thank you all for coming here on such short notice."

The five men and one woman seated around the small conference room table nodded and each uttered their own version of, "of course, governor".

"I do not need to say this and it will become clear in a moment, but I will plead with you now to keep everything we discuss in confidence. You ultimately may not sign on to what we are about to discuss, but I have asked you all here today not because I expect you to follow me, but rather because I consider you trusted advisors, who want what is best for this state and for this country. David, you are here for a very specific reason that will become clear after Mr. Tanner explains why we are here." Beachum then looked at Tanner, "Billy, want don't you start us off?"

Tanner looking slightly surprised, smiled at the governor and then looked around at the others seated at the table. "The governor has decided that the Roe decision goes too far. He's decided that we have no choice but to invoke, ummm, the nuclear option."

Nancy Carson looked around at the rest in a slightly amused way. "Secede? You are talking about secession?"

"Yes, that's what he's talking about. Bill and I have discussed it and I have decided that we have bent over long enough and this latest affront to what we believe in and more importantly, those who elected me believe in, requires something, ummm, radical."

Scott Rumphy, living every bit up to his nickname of "Rumples", quickly interjected. "Governor, excuse my French, but this is nuts."

"Fuck that, Rumples. Ahh, sorry, Governor." Beachum nodded at his Comptroller, Rick Newsome. "But everything we have lived through over the past seven-years has been fucking nuts. We have a President who has twice been elected by less than half the voters, a Congress that repeatedly gets elected by less than half the voters, but has redrawn every map guaranteeing the outcome with the signoff of a Supreme Court, which claims to be originalists only when it suits their agenda, and they govern to the agenda of the minority and we just sit there and fucking take it!" He gagged on the last part of his diatribe, a result of his getting too worked up.

Rumphy stared at Newsome for two beats. "It is nuts, Rick. I get everything you just said and I agree with all of it. The system is broken and the other side is almost literally dancing on our graves, but to suggest that the solution is to effectively start the second American Civil War is ludicrous."

Fred Pugliano, the state's Lieutenant Governor, now chimed in. "I'm with Rumples. I hate everything they represent and I hate how we are unable to do much of anything about it, but when we talked about secession, I thought we were, I don't know, messing around."

Beachum looked at his Lieutenant. He had known Fred Pugliano for most of his 51-years. They had grown up four houses apart in a suburb of San Diego and had attended most of the same schools, including USC – Fred on a football scholarship, Beachum on an academic scholarship. Pugliano was the toughest son-of-a-bitch Beachum had ever met and not one to ever shy away from a good fight.

"Freddie, when have you ever known me to mess around?"

"Fuck it, I'm in," replied Pugliano.

Beachum laughed out loud and soon the others joined him. Not only was Pugliano the toughest SOB Beachum had ever met, but also one of the funniest.

Beachum then paused for a while and the others stared back at him expectantly. "Look, I realize this step is not only the nuclear option, but also probably the end of my political career and maybe ultimately my freedom. But, and you need to all understand this – Jill has been dead for eight years and every night I go to sleep thinking about what she would think of all this and what she would want me to do."

"She'd tell you to stop being "retahded" in that thick fuckin' Boston accent of hers and get to sleep."

"Maybe Freddie, maybe. But I don't think so. I think she'd listen to my lamenting about what's going on every day and every night and she'd eventually say – "stop ya whining and do something about it."" Beachum did the last part in his own version of Jill's accent and then paused for a moment. His face betrayed the memory of her loss. "And that's what I'm going to do."

Beachum now turned to his chief legal counsel, David Walters. "David? You've been awfully quiet, tell me how to do this?"

Walters cleaned his glasses with a white handkerchief. He did so meticulously and it was "the tell" for when he was considering his answer. He was in his early 40s, wore a $5,000 dark blue

Zegna suit and was the most handsome man Beachum had ever met. A tall order considering Beachum was the Governor of California.

"I wasn't quite prepared for this and you will appreciate that I have not boned up on my Constitutional Law as it relates to the issue of state's rights and the issues of dis-union."

Beachum interrupted, "but."

Walters allowed himself a small smile. "But, recalling my Harvard days," he said this part not to boast, but simply to advance his answer. "I think the law is fairly well-settled on this issue of secession and more specifically that the Constitution was established to be a permanent union and secession by its very nature is anathema to this." Walters paused.

"But?"

Walters looked at Beachum and stared for two beats. "There really is not a "but" as it relates to the issue of secession." He paused again. "But and this was articulated by both President James Madison and by the Supreme Court that while secession is impossible, revolution against intolerable oppression under our Constitution is not."

Pugliano made a face and purposely tried to sound like a New York tough guy, "revolution, huh."

The room sat silent for a moment. Nancy Carson then weighed in. "So legally, how would you do this?"

Walters was cleaning his glasses again. "Miss Carson, Mr. Pugliano, Mr. Tanner, Governor Beachum, Rumples ..." His formality followed by his use of Rumples caused the others to laugh, albeit nervously.

He continued. "As I said, I will need to research this further, but I don't think the law is ever going to be entirely on our side." Beachum smiled to himself, he liked that Walters had said "our" as he liked having him on their side.

"However, I do not think anything prevents us from putting the question on the ballot, as long as we make a point of using the language outlined by the Founding Fathers. It may ultimately not be legal, but as we have learned in this current day and age, that may not matter in the end."

The room was again silent for a while and then Nancy Carson spoke. "Okay, governor, what's the plan?"

Beachum smiled. "Billy suggested that I just announce it, Nancy. Something like," Beachum read from a piece of paper he pulled from his inside jacket pocket, "The state of California, which represents 12% of this nation's population and 15% of this nation's economic activity can no longer stand for the intolerable oppression." Beachum purposely inserted Walters' language. Walters did not react.

Beachum continued. "intolerable oppression that is being suffered upon it from a Federal government that was elected by a minority vote. While I appreciate the value of this great democracy and how it has endured over the past 250-years, I also think that it has been completely bastardized over the past decade. Simply – our Founding Fathers did not foresee this and, in fact, warned of intolerable oppression and the need for revolution when faced with it. "Beachum again looked at Walters, who this time nodded.

He continued. "And as we saw with other periods of history where enlightened men and women stood by in the face of repeated injustice, California will not sit idly by. We are better than that and this country is better than that. And if this great democracy is meant to endure, we must take a stand against the repeated Federal injustices being wrought upon us. As such, today, I announce that the state of California will hold a vote this November in which the question will be asked –

are you in favor of remaining as part of these United States of America or are you in favor of seceding and forming the country of California where the freedoms and principles of our Founding Fathers will be respected."

The room sat silent.

"Excuse my French again, but holy shit, get a damned speech writer, would you please?"

The seven people around the table laughed. "Fair enough, Rumples, fair enough. Billy and I don't have your polish with the pen. But that's the gist of it."

"What happens after?"

They all turned to look at Pugliano. Who took a sip of water and then continued. "Okay, so you announce California is going to vote on secession or revolution or however we frame it and it's, ummm, four months until Election Day. What do you think happens next?"

Beachum turned and nodded toward Tanner. "Bill?"

Tanner ran his hand through his hair. He had been blessed with a full mane and he often relished in running his hands through it as an act of machismo.

"The Governor and I talked about that and in light of what David laid out - there's no precedence for something like this. At least not one that's less than 150-years old. Add to that how batshit crazy the President can be and it makes it even harder to peg."

Nancy interrupted, "He could order the army in. Or order the FBI to arrest you."

They all turned to look at her. She continued, "I think those are real possibilities. Order you arrested and if that doesn't work because we would essentially have your protection detail and the state police pitted against the FBI, he orders in the army to take control."

"Or he could go the constitutional route." They all turned to look at Walters. After 30-seconds of quiet, the laughter began again. Even Walters allowed himself to laugh.

"Yeah, this guy is going to take the measured approach." They all continued to laugh as Pugliano weighed in.

"What about other states?" They all stopped laughing.

They turned to Rumphy. "I mean, we are not unique in how we feel about what's happening. How do you think New York reacts?"

Beachum looked at all their faces with a slight smile on his face. "I've already made that call."

7

June 15th, 2018

San Diego, California

"You bought him a bat?"

Larry smiled sheepishly. His son stared up at him from just below Larry's right knee. The boy tried to hold the handle of the bat with the barrel sitting on the floor; although the bat was at least a foot taller than he was. "He said that's what he wanted."

Larry looked down at Cody, who looked back at his dad and nodded. "Larry, he's two. He barely says anything that makes any sense and you decided he said he wanted a bat for his birthday?" Beth shifted in the hospital bed, the baby held to her right breast, continuing to feed heartily.

"I resent that Beth and I think Cody does too. He said he wanted a bat and who am I to stand in the way of the next Mike Trout?"

"So he said, hey dad, I would like a bat for my birthday?"

"No, he said, hey Larry, I would like a bat for my birthday – we are still working on the dad thing."

Beth sighed. "Funny guy." And then, her attention shifted to the television that was mounted against the wall above Larry's right shoulder.

Larry turned and although the sound was muted, it was easy to see what was going on. It was more footage from the border. Kids literally being ripped from their parents arms. It then cut back to the Fox News studio and although there was no sound, Larry knew that the "newscasters" were putting some spin on what was happening that made it seem like all of this was somehow okay.

Beth sighed again. "Quite a world we're bringing this one into." Beth motioned to the small baby that was attached to her left breast.

Larry reached up and turned off the television. "Things will get better. I think we have to go through a cleansing like this every so often. The whole country goes nuts for a while and then realizes that the old normal was better. Rinse, wash, repeat - until we do it again 30 or 40 years from now.

Beth bit her lip, which Larry knew to take as a signal that she was about to disagree with him. "This time feels different. You've got what is essentially a small minority of this country – disgruntled white people who don't live on a coast

– who are reshaping this system to their world view. Going to be hard to shift that back."

"Can we not talk about this now? Especially with him going to town on your boob?"

Beth looked down at the baby. "Ba ba rainbow." Both Beth and Larry looked down at Cody, who had become transfixed by a picture of a rainbow on the wall. Although he had pronounced it "rain-ow".

"You see? He said "bat".

Beth looked at Larry and then at Cody. "If you say so."

8

July 8th, 2023

Albany, New York

"He's doing what?"

New York Governor Brenda Cossimo leaned back in her chair and stared across her desk at her top aide. "He's going to announce that California is going to hold a vote in November in which seceding from the Union is on the ballot. I mean, he's not going to quite call it that – revolution in the face of intolerable oppression is what their legal guys are recommending - but it's essentially secession."

Debbie Messimer stared at the Governor. "That's crazy and frankly awesome at the same time. God, I wish I could see the President's face the moment Beachum announces that."

Cossimo turned her head to stare out the window lost in thought. "I imagine the Oval Office is going to need some repair after that speech." They both laughed. "So, Debra – what do you really think?"

Messimer squinted at the Governor. "I'm not sure I get what you mean?"

Cossimo continued. "Well, California is I imagine going to secede or whatever they are calling it because the state hates what is happening as much as its Governor does. Many in this state feel the same way, do we just sit idly by and see what happens or do we …" She let the last words sit there.

Messimer cut in. "Do we what? Join them? Holy crap – that would be amazing. I would love to be a part of that. But I am also pretty sure that it ends with both of us," she paused for a beat, "or at least you in jail when all is said and done. But gosh, I would kill to be a part of that."

Cossimo nodded. She appreciated the youthful enthusiasm of her much younger aide. "Who can we trust?"

Messimer stared at the Governor for several beats. "George for sure. He'd run through a fuckin' wall for you. Stacy and Sully wouldn't take the wall, but they'd at least knock down the door. Maybe Brinson, but he has leaky sails, so I'm not sure you want to let him know before Beachum gives his speech."

Cossimo held up a piece of paper that had been sitting on the desk in front of her. It had Debbie Messimer, George Deacon, Stacy Silver and Mike Sullivan listed as the first four names with Terry Brinson's name below with a line through it. "What is it they say about great minds?"

Messimer smiled. "So what's the play?"

Cossimo sighed. "I think we meet at my place under dark of night and we let them in on what's going to happen. We then spitball about how New York responds to this."

Messimer smiled again. "Love the cloak and dagger. But what I meant was, absent meeting with them, what is your gut tell you the play is for New York?"

Cossimo turned to stare at the window again. She squinted as a Lexus SUV turned into the driveway of the Governor's mansion. Alex and Remy were home. "What is it that Churchill said – "I never worry about action, but only about inaction." Or something like that." Cossimo paused again. "I feel like all we've done over the past few years is inaction. Let's give action a try."

Messimer stared back at the Governor, her mouth now slightly agape. "Awesome, truly fucking awesome."

9

June 29th, 2034

Long Beach, California

Larry backed up the forklift and then brought it forward, effortlessly lowering the forks just in time to slide under the next load. He then drove the Class 5 lift forward and carried the three-ton load to the stacks, which were 40-meters to the right. Larry's head hurt. He had spent the last two nights "surveying" and catching what sleep he could underneath the same copse of trees that he and Karen had hidden three nights before.

He had surveyed his place, of course. The gestapo was well hidden, but they were there. Larry had already staked out a spot several years before to survey his place in case the world ever decided to close in on a former member of America's most wanted.

Two blocks away and on the opposite side of the street from his apartment was a doorway that had a recess off to its right. The recess had a small step in it, which elevated Larry about 12-inches above street level. From there and with the help of some cheap binoculars Larry had bought from a pawn shop the morning after "the incident", he could see his apartment and most of what was happening on that side of the street. The gestapo didn't advertise its presence, but one man sat behind the wheel of a car just up the street and Larry was certain he could make out a second in his apartment, who had a tendency to check the window every few minutes.

Larry had also spent some time surveying 14 Wesson – the place that Karen had mentioned to him. If the government guys were good, whoever was residing at 14 Wesson were better. No one checked the windows and no one came or went – at least as far as Larry could notice from a doorway across the street. That said – he was pretty sure there were people inside.

While the shades were drawn and the lights were dim, he got a sense that something was moving inside and he felt that it was more than one person. As he often was, Larry was reminded of something from years ago as he stared across the street at the quiet windows of 14 Wesson. He didn't spend long reminiscing as the curfew was still in effect and he was on unfamiliar turf, but he left satisfied that whatever Karen was, she wasn't trying to set him up with an ambush.

After he deposited the load, Larry turned the lift and prepared to repeat the feat. "Stabler, you got a second?"

Larry looked across at his foreman, Jack Kennex, who stood just outside his trailer about 30-yards from Larry. Larry tapped his helmet, which was a signal to Kennex that he'd be down momentarily and he then drove the forklift forward to deposit it in the parking depot.

Three minutes later, Larry opened the door to the trailer. Kennex hung up the phone as Larry walked in and signaled for him to sit down. Kennex was a bear of a man with thick arms and a solid frame. Larry had little doubt that back in the day, Kennex would have made a better friend than foe and even at what looked to be close to 60, Kennex still cut a menacing figure. "How are things, Larry?"

Larry sat and shrugged. "Okay. Same, I guess."

Kennex studied Larry for a couple of beats. "Can I ask you a question?"

Larry looked at Kennex. In the four years he had worked at the docks, he was unsure as to whether he had ever had a conversation this long with the man. Larry made a point of doing his job and keeping to himself and Kennex seemed to respect that. "Shoot."

Kennex stared back at Larry. He seemed unsure of how to ask the question. After a pause, "you were military, right?"

Larry tried not to portray any emotion. "What makes you ask?"

Kennex sat back in his chair. "I was military. Second infantry in Afghanistan, 30-years ago. And then in the invasion …" Kennex's voice trailed off for a moment. "You get a sense for someone who carries themselves in that way. You have that way."

Larry already suspected about Kennex's past, but he still portrayed surprise. "Afghanistan? Man, what was that like?"

Kennex didn't quite take the bait. "You didn't answer the question, but okay. It was a shithole and those fuckers hid IEDs anywhere they could." He then paused in reflection for a moment. "But I wouldn't trade that time for anything that came before or since."

Larry stared at Kennex. "That must have been tough. That how you hurt your leg?" Kennex walked with a noticeable, albeit slight limp.

Kennex stared back at Larry and then smiled. "Man, you really don't take the bait. Okay, I'm going to say you are military because I am fifty fuckin' seven years old and I have been through enough shit in this life to know the measure of a man." He then paused for two beats. "I'm going to tell you right now that I am on your side."

Larry stared back at him. He then ran his right hand through his hair, reflexively pausing on a scar hidden beneath his greying and somewhat thinning red mane just at the top of his head. "I'm not sure what you mean."

Kennex stared back. "I have some friends, Larry, who'd like to meet you. They think very highly of what you've done. Call this a crazy fuckin' coincidence or just that you are ridiculously unlucky, but what you did the other night happened to effect someone I hold very dear, and they wanted you to know that you don't need to sleep in Klein Park."

Larry did not betray any emotion, but rather looked at the door to the trailer. He instantly realized this was an amateur move. Kennex looked over at the door, seemingly aware of what Larry was thinking.

"You can go if that's what you want. You don't need to bolt for the door because I'm too fuckin' old to chase you and from the story I heard about the other night, you'd probably snap my neck with your left pinky."

Larry stared for two beats and then gave a half smile. "My right maybe. The left is my weak side."

Kennex smiled and sat back again, looking more comfortable. He laced his fingers behind his head and then said, "I've been instructed to ask you to come to 14 Wesson. We already know that you know where it is as you have been there the last two nights. We are sure that it's safe, even though we keep a low profile about the place, so before curfew tonight, come knock on the door."

Larry began to contemplate all of his professional training. He realized from Kennex's confession that whatever Larry's skills once were, a fair bit of rust had apparently gathered in his recon abilities.

After several moments in which neither man spoke, Kennex said, "now get the fuck back to work."

10

February 4th, 2009

Kabul, Afghanistan

The Red Bear stood in the shadows, looking through his night vision goggles at the window across the street. The blinds were drawn and those inside were professional enough to stay clear of the window. The light inside was dim, so shadows were not obvious. Just in front of the Red Bear, Daxx and Nugget continued to crouch to the side of a parked car, which looked like it had been built a century earlier and not cleaned since.

"Movement," whispered the Red Bear. No one had come to the window, nor had he seen shadows move per se, but he was now certain there were people inside.

Daxx and Nugget both silently chambered rounds and then Daxx said, "what's the play?"

The Red Bear removed his goggles and crouched next to them, checking his watch. Looking across the street at the window, the Red Bear whispered, "we have to assume the package is in there, so we are green lit. If he's not, then we are going to have some splanin' to do."

Daxx and Nugget both nodded. "Daxxy, you come in from behind the red car. Nugget, you cut in front of this rusty bucket. I'm going to come in low and straight across. We meet at the outer door."

While the plan lacked art, it was the straight ahead attack that the Red Bear tended to favor, so neither Daxx nor Nugget were surprised. Daxx left first because he had the longest route. He got in position behind the red car and then the Red Bear made a beeline for the door, staying low with his M4 carbine in the ready fire position. They arrived almost simultaneously and Daxx quickly removed his small tool kit from his left breast pocket. Within seconds, the door was open, revealing a small foyer and a stairway leading up into the battle scarred building.

The Red Bear took point, as he always did and the three made their way up the stairs, coming to the second floor landing, which had three doors. The Red Bear pointed at the one on the left, light peaking from beneath.

Daxx again got into place, silently picking the two locks that secured the door. He then nodded and backed away and the Red Bear silently pointed at Nugget and the stairway and then the floor. Nugget instantly understood and backed up to the stairs, laying flat on the floor, his M4 pointed at the still closed door.

The Red Bear quietly opened the door, revealing a short hallway with the ambient light of a room at its end. The only thing visible from the room was its opposite wall, which was bare. Voices could be heard, but not made out from their position.

The Red Bear looked at the two men and silently pounded his right fist into his left hand. They both nodded and Nugget rose to his feet; although he stayed behind the other two.

The Red Bear had to admit that he didn't like it. Ideally, the door would have opened into the room and Nugget would have silently taken out anyone in plain sight with the Red Bear and Daxx cleaning up those that were not visible from Nugget's position. But this set-up was going to require what he liked to call "the bull rush."

The Red Bear took a deep breath and then sprinted down the hallway of the apartment. He hit the space opening up into the room and saw two men sitting on the couch. He recognized one as the package – the scar on his right cheek was a dead giveaway – and he quickly shot the other between the eyes. The package gasped and another man wandered into the room from what must have been the kitchen. Daxx, who had followed two steps behind the Red Bear, shot the man coming from the kitchen twice in the chest. He died before he hit the floor. Daxx then crossed behind the Red

Bear and did a quick check of the room from where the fallen man had just come, whispering "clear" when he had finished his inspection.

One other door sat next to the couch where the package sat. The Red Bear held up one finger to his lips and the package seemed to get the point. Daxx looked at the door and quickly made a decision. He flicked his M4 to automatic and fired a volley of silenced rounds into the door and the wall, coming within inches of where the package sat with his final volley.

He then pushed open the door, which had lost its latch in Daxx's volley and did a quick inspection. At the foot of a bed lay a dead woman, an AK47 limply held in her arms. "Clear," he whispered.

The Red Bear looked down the hall and whispered, "clear." He then made his way across to the package and without hesitating, took a syringe from his breast pocket, removing the plastic tip with a flick of his thumb and injected the package in the neck. The package gasped, but within seconds he became sluggish and 30-seconds later he was unconscious. The Red Bear fluidly lifted him over his shoulder and he and Daxx exited the apartment.

90-seconds later, the three army rangers and their package were back at their vehicle – a nondescript

1975 Chevy Impala. The drive back to base was quiet; although, Daxx drove as though a caravan of enemy troops were in pursuit. Along the way, they saw the lights of other vehicles down various side streets, but the Red Bear had a gut feeling that they had pulled off the extraction without raising any alarms.

15-minutes after they exited the apartment with the package, the Red Bear stood before Colonel Jim Davies. Davies was roughly half the size of the Red Bear, but very much a razor blade of a man – sharp edges, never a speck of visible dirt or a crease in his uniform. While the Red Bear could probably best him in a fight, his gut told him that he would leave the encounter worse for the wear.

"I have to say, this was some of your better work."

"Thank you, sir. I couldn't have done it without Daxton and Howard, sir."

Colonel Davies looked across his desk, evaluating the man he had come to respect, but not really know over the past nine-months. "I'm sure you couldn't and I will make sure that HQ gets word of how they availed themselves."

The Red Bear nodded. An awkward silence descended upon the room. The Red Bear continued to stand with his hands folded behind him, while Davies sat at his desk. Davies knew that he could tell the Red Bear to relax, but he would continue to stand as he was. Davies then looked at the side door to his office and then back at the Red Bear.

The larger man took note of what his CO had done, but his training told him not to betray his knowledge by looking at the door himself. After 20-seconds more of silence, Davies spoke. "There are some gentlemen here who would like to speak with you."

The Red Bear was silent for two beats, expecting more from Davies and then, "sir?"

Davies continued. "You don't have to speak with them as I am pretty sure they are CIA and they are looking to recruit you and despite all the clandestine bullshit you read about in books, you can say no and no one is going to hold it against you."

The Red Bear continued to stare at Davies. He appreciated his CO's candor, which was rare in the world of the military or frankly the world in general. "What do you think I should do, sir?"

Davies sat back in his chair and contemplated the Red Bear's question for a moment. "I think I have known you for less than a year and I already couldn't imagine doing this job without you. I also think your buddies Daxton and Howard are very capable and have learned a tremendous amount from working with you, so we'd probably find a way to get by."

The Red Bear shifted his feet and nodded to Davies.

"Listen to what they have to say. You have got the skills and the head to go very far in this, ummm, industry. If you don't like what you hear, politely decline."

The Bear nodded again. "Thank you, sir."

Davies sat forward. "No thanks are necessary." As the Red Bear moved toward the side door, Davies said, "good luck, Larry."

11

May 20th, 2021

Fairfax, Virginia

Judith Rosenberg sat staring at the screen on her small laptop. She reread what she had written for the fourth time, now satisfied that she had not made any obvious grammatical faux pas. While the letter was only 293 words, her fingers still ached a bit – the cost of being 89-years young as she liked to remind her children.

She sat back for moment and decided one more read was warranted. When she had finished, she removed her glasses and pinched her nose between her eyes to help the inevitable rush she got when removing her glasses. She then reached forward and hit the print button, activating the printer to the left of her desk.

After removing the single page from her printer, she returned to her desk and leaned over to give the letter one more read, this time aloud:

Dear Mr. President,

This letter acts as a formal notification of my decision, effective ten days hence – May 30th, 2021, to end my regular active status as an Associate Justice of the United States Supreme

Court, while continuing to serve in a senior status, as provided in 28 U.S.C 371 (b).

It has been my profound honor to serve this country and I wish to thank all of my colleagues on the Court – some living, some not – for not only their dedication to service, but also to the rule of law. While we have not always seen eye to eye and I have often found myself writing for the minority, I retire with nothing but deep respect for those that I have worked with over the past quarter century.

Mr. President, while it is not necessarily my place to make recommendations to you on my replacement, I urge you to consider the make-up not only of this great body, but also the make-up of the country at large. We live in deeply divided times. Much of the population, perhaps even a majority, feels that this Court has become deeply politicized over the past decade with a growing number of originalists replacing what the media likes to describe as "moderate" justices.

While I would hope that your ultimate choice will be guided by who is most qualified for the position, I fear that this may not be the case and that politics rather than jurisprudence will guide the decision. I would urge you to lean on the latter rather than the former, as the implications for this country and how it is governed not only over your and my lifetimes, but also for generations to come, are at stake.

God bless the United States of America.

Respectfully,

Judith Harriette Rosenberg

Without hesitation, Rosenberg signed the letter and then sat back again in her chair. She turned to stare out her home office window. Her garden needed some work, something she imagined she would have more time for with the time she had left.

She had tried to hold on. In the wake of the 2016 election, she had told herself that she could hold out for four more years, despite the aches and pains that increasingly festooned her day and her mind's tendency to start to wander. When Ryerson retired in 2018 and the Court makeup took a definitive turn, her fortitude for remaining in the position only increased, even though her ability to concentrate for long periods continued to worsen day by day.

She had awoken on the morning of Wednesday November 4th to the news that the President had been reelected by the narrowest of Electoral College victories, despite losing the popular vote by nearly five million votes. She had known that morning that her "quest to survive" as she liked to call it to her closest confidantes was at an end. She would make it through her final term, but she would not outlast this President after-all.

She place the letter in an envelope that simply read "Mr. President" and then picked up the phone on her desk. "Tommy, would you come in here please?"

After she had handed the letter to her assistant and given him explicit instructions, he left the room, leaving her once again alone with her thoughts. She sat silently for about a minute and then leaned forward, opening up a new email on her computer.

She entered the email addresses for the editors of the New York Times, the Washington Post, the Boston Globe and the Chicago Tribune – all of which Thomas "Tommy" Penderson had gotten for her the day before. She then typed into the subject line "To whom it may concern" and attached the letter she had just written.

While she did not like being a political animal, she had decided that morning to send out the letter at the same time she dispatched it to the White House. Call it one last act of defiance in a life that had generally been played pretty close to the vest.

Without hesitating she hit "Send" and sat back again in her chair. God bless us indeed.

12

July 21, 1987

Moscow, Soviet Union

"Dimitri report."

Dimitri Restanov adjusted his tie and looked at the KGB's number two man in its Political Intelligence Department. "I think it went as expected, Deputy Kruschoff."

Vladimir Kruschoff nodded. "Give me details."

Dimitri smiled. "We put him in the Lenin Suite as discussed and made sure he got a taste of the finer things that Moscow has to offer."

"Go on."

"We then took him to some of the potential development sites. We do not expect that anything will come of it, but we did learn quite a bit about how he responds to flattery."

"And?" Kruschoff leaned forward in anticipation.

Dimitri smiled. "I would say and the Ambassador agrees that he is extremely susceptible to flattery and may be driven by nothing other than pure greed."

Kruschoff nodded and then paused in thought. "And politically? Would you say he has ambitions?"

Dimitri nodded. "He was quite critical of President Reagan and decried the way that Japan was stealing America."

"And did we plant any seeds?"

Dimitri smiled again. "Of course, Deputy Kruschoff. We saw an opportunity to press him on the issue of Japan and pointed out how much the United States wastes every year on defending a country that is stealing from it."

Kruschoff smiled and nodded. "That's good, Dimitri. You have done well." Kruschoff reached into his desk and removed a bottle of vodka. He poured glasses for the both of them and then passed one to Dimitri.

"To cultivating new relationships."

They raised their glasses.

13

June 29th, 2034

Los Angeles, California

Larry stood at the corner, focusing on the building across the street. Despite the warm Los Angeles night, he wore a light jacket and the same pair of jeans and a tee shirt he had been wearing the night he met Karen.

Larry knew there was no point to trying to hide his position as he thought he had done that quite effectively the past two evenings and yet Kennex had made it clear that they knew exactly what he was up to. Speakers to the right of him blared "the curfew will begin in 10 minutes".

Three minutes later, Larry stood in front of the door. Aware that standing there could potentially attract attention he knocked twice. Seconds later the door opened, it was Kennex.

"Larry, I'm glad you came. Come in."

Larry entered and the two men faced each other in a small foyer. The two men stood there for a moment and Larry wondered briefly whether Kennex would search him. The man made no move to pat him down and instead pointed to his right. A staircase led up and Larry was reminded of a prior mission – was he the package this time?

Larry followed Kennex up the stairs and the two men entered a much larger room. All of the furniture had been set up well away from the windows and the blinds were drawn. Two men sat on a large couch, while Larry could hear activity coming from another room. The two men rose, Larry instantly recognized the one on the left.

Kennex held out his arm toward the men. "Larry Stabler, I'd like you to meet Ken Dougherty and Phil Richards."

Larry met the men half way, his hand extended. "Ken, Phil."

Richards shook his hand first and then Dougherty. He held Larry's hand longer than he should have, seemingly studying Larry's face. "Have we met before, Larry?"

Larry stared back at him, his face taking on a skeptical look. "I don't think so, Ken."

Dougherty stared back. "You sure? You seem really fuckin' familiar to me."

Larry half shrugged and half shook his head. Richards then interceded. "I'm pretty sure Larry would remember meeting someone as fucking ugly as you, Kenny."

The two men gave halfhearted laughs and then a woman entered the room carrying a tray of sandwiches – it was Karen. She gave a broad smile when she saw Larry. "Larry, you made it."

Larry had to admit that he felt a stir unlike anything he had felt in more than a decade. He returned her smile, albeit more sheepishly.

Karen put the tray down on a table in front of the couch and without hesitating, embraced Larry in a deep hug. The stir had now become something more profound.

Larry did not at first return the embrace, but he then encircled Karen for two beats before discreetly ending their embrace.

"She never hugs me like that."

Dougherty replied, "because you smell, Philly."

The two men and Kennex laughed, while Karen and Larry continued to stare at one another.

After a brief uncomfortable silence, Kennex interjected, "why don't we sit and eat and catch up?"

Dougherty and Richards took their seats again on the couch, while Larry, Karen and Kennex grabbed chairs on the other side of the small coffee table where Karen had placed the sandwiches. Without asking, Dougherty, Richards and Kennex grabbed a sandwich, while Karen and Larry sat and observed.

"So, Larry, tell us about yourself."

The room sat silent and then Kennex snorted, letting out a laugh. "Nice try, Philly." The others seemed to let a collective breath out, as the tension had been momentarily tamed.

Larry looked around at the others. "Not really much to tell."

Kennex looked at Dougherty and Richards and then at Karen. They all expected, hoped, that Larry would say more. "You really aren't much of a conversationalist, Larry."

Larry studied the other four. He then nonchalantly stretched out his left leg, closer to the coffee table. "Not really. Let's just say that this crazy world we live in doesn't make me want to be much of a sharer."

"Why did you open the door the other night, Larry? Doesn't seem like the sort of thing someone who doesn't like to share would want to do."

Larry stared at Karen. "I'm not sure." Larry then kicked out his left leg, knocking the coffee table into Dougherty and Richards, who reflexively threw up their hands to deflect not only the table, but the flying sandwiches. Larry then drew two guns from inside his jacket, one his Glock from the other night and the other a small Sig Sauer P230 that he had gotten from the same pawnshop where he bought the binoculars. He slowly got up from the chair, backing away.

He leveled one of the guns at Dougherty and Richards, who were picking bits of meat and bread from their faces. He pointed the other at Kennex. Karen wore tight black jeans and a tee shirt. Based on her outfit, he was fairly certain she was unarmed.

Larry said nothing but kept the guns trained on the three men.

After a couple of beats, Kennex motioned with his hands. "Calm down, Larry."

Larry looked at Kennex. "Do I seem not calm?"

Kennex laughed. "Aside from pointing two guns at us, I guess you do seem pretty calm."

Larry, betraying no emotion, looked at Karen while he kept the two guns trained at the three men. "Do you doubt that I will kill these men if they try anything?"

Karen looked at Kennex and then at Dougherty. He had a slice of tomato across the bridge of his nose that he had somehow missed. She then looked at Larry. "No, I don't."

Larry stared at her for two beats. "Why is that?"

She seemed surprised by the question. "I'm not sure I follow, Larry."

Larry stared at her for nearly thirty seconds. "I have to say that you are either the luckiest woman ever to walk the face of this earth or the trickiest."

Karen stared back at him, squinting a bit when he said "trickiest". "I'm still not sure I follow."

"Larry, why don't we talk this .."

"Shut the fuck up, Jack." Larry's voice remained calm as he looked at Kennex and then back at Karen.

"Okay, I'll start, Karen. I have lived my life with the general belief in two things. One, coincidences happen, but they are exceedingly rare, so too many coincidences is probably something else."

Larry paused and the room sat silent for a moment. "And the second?"

Larry turned to Richards, who now seemed to regret having asked a question. Larry looked back at Karen. "My gut is generally pretty reliable." Larry felt a certain bit of internal pain when the said this. While he didn't think it had registered on his face, he wasn't sure.

Karen stared at him. "And what does your gut tell you, Larry?

Larry stared back for three beats. "You had five buildings on my side of the street, including two doors that were closer than my building. I saw you come across the street and you ran at least thirty feet further than you needed to in order to get to my building. You then had twenty apartment doors you could have knocked on and you knocked on mine. Dumb luck for you and for me? Maybe. But then my boss, who has literally said fourteen words to me over the past three-and-a-half years, happens to know you and somehow connects you with me and all of a sudden we are getting to an awful lot of concurrent coincidences, which is violating my number one golden rule."

Karen stared back at him. "And your gut?"

For the first time, Larry showed some emotion, betraying a brief smile. "My gut tells me that I am being set-up for something."

"Does your gut tell you that we are bad people?"

Larry stared back at Karen and studied her face. "Not yet."

14

June 27th, 2034

Los Angeles, California

Karen looked at her watch and then at Dougherty, Richards and Anderson. "You ready?"

The three men nodded and Karen took off running across the street. Dougherty fired three times, purposely missing above her head, hitting the side of a building, just below its second floor windows. Richards then fired four times as Karen rounded the corner, hitting a parked car just behind her. When she was around the corner, the three men set off in pursuit. Anderson yelled out, "stop running!"

Karen ran two blocks down Sunset and reached Reardon Drive. She again checked her watch, waited fifteen-seconds and then bolted diagonally across the street as two more shots hit the lamp post three feet to her right. "Jesus assholes, not so fucking close," she silently whispered to herself.

Karen reached the door in seconds and pushed her way in. As she entered, five more shots exploded against the façade of the building. Not hesitating, she quickly ascended to the third floor and briefly stood outside apartment 32. She took a deep

breath and then tapped lightly on the door.
"Please, I need help."

15

July 10th, 2023

Somewhere over the Atlantic Ocean

President of the United States, Richard Champer, his Chief of Staff, Cal Doggett, the Vice-President of the United States, Peter Partridge, and the Commerce Secretary, William Saskins III, sat aboard Air Force 1. They all stared intently at the screen in the main boardroom.

"He's going to announce he's running."

"You'll crush him, Petey. Boring Beachum will put 'em to sleep if he even gets the nomination." Champer nodded as he said this to his Vice-President. Something in Champer's eyes seemed a bit disingenuous to Partridge.

The Vice-President smiled; although, it was very much the fake smile he had learned to display any time the President spoke. "For sure, Mr. President."

The two turned back to the television as Beachum began to speak. "Ladies and Gentlemen, great citizens of California, I stand before you today very much at a crossroads." The crowd that had been estimated at around 10,000 fell silent. Someone from the crowd yelled out, "we love you,

Governor." Smatterings of laughter could be heard and applause briefly broke out."

Beachum paused, looking down at the notes in front of him. He had decided because of the sensitive nature of his speech not to use the teleprompter, but rather to read from his notes. "And I love you as well, which is truly what brings me before you on this beautiful morning."

Again more applause. After the crowd quieted, Beachum stared out at the multitude of faces. "Over these past seven years, I have stood by and watched as many of the things I hold dear have been ripped apart. From environmental regulations to the treatment of women and minorities to the ostracizing of those who would seek a better life in this country to the great wall that as we speak is under construction on our southern border. These are only but a sampling of the myriad of wrongs that I have watched, often feeling helpless to do much about them." Beachum paused and looked at the crowd, which stood nearly completely silent.

"Were these affronts to what I hold true perpetrated by the will of the people, I think then that I would have reluctantly accepted them. However, this is sadly not the case. Half of the past six elections have seen the elected president receive less than half of the popular vote. This is not fake news or the work of some secret subplot as our current President and his sycophants with Fox News have repeatedly suggested, but rather an undeniable truth."

Beachum turned to stare at the Fox News cameras as the completed the last line. "A more humble man, a more righteous man, aware that he was elected not once, but twice with support from less than have of the population of this great nation, would undoubtedly tailor his agenda not to the minority that elected him, but rather to the whole country, thankful and respectful of the opportunity that our electoral system afforded him. But this sadly has not been the case. Not by matters of degree, but rather by matters of magnitude. Quite simply – we have what can only be described as the most one-sided Federal government in our history. One that cares little for the will of the majority, but rather governs solely for the minority, despite the fact it was essentially elected on a technicality."

Champer turned to his advisors. The anger on his face was obvious. The three other men continued to stare at the television, afraid to make eye contact.

"Our Founding Fathers set up a system of checks and balances perhaps precisely because of the risks we face today. However, our Congress, also elected by a minority of the population and empowered by a Supreme Court that allows electoral maps to be redrawn and gerrymandered - thus insuring that the minority will continue to maintain its hold on power. Congress has completely ignored the duty assigned to it by our Founding Fathers, rendering not only our Constitution moot, but also all the principles we hold dear."

Beachum paused and looked over the crowd. The moment of truth was upon him and rather than feeling nerves, he felt a sense of calm wash over him. "Citizens of California, we will stand for this no longer. We will no longer stand for the destruction of our environment. We will no longer stand for the demonization of the immigrants that helped build this country. We will no longer stand for racism toward minority groups. We will no longer stand for the desecration of women. And we will not stand for a federal government and a Supreme Court that would criminalize a woman's right to choose. This intolerable oppression cannot stand."

With each statement, the cheers of the crowd grew with the last one eliciting the loudest roar from those assembled.

"Citizens of California, today we take a stand. Today, we turn words in to action."

"Here it comes." The President, who continued to look like he had just gone ten rounds with a heavyweight boxer, sat forward in his seat. "He's running."

"Today, I announce that on this November the sixth, of this year two thousand and twenty-three, you will be faced with one question on the ballot. Revolution against intolerable oppression under the guise of secession for the state of California from these United States or continued membership in this once great Union. It is a decision that I would urge you not to take lightly, but one that I believe is the right and only just thing to do until the injustices of our broken system are repaired."

"What the fuck is he doing?" Champer gripped the edge of the table. "Can we cut him off? Can we shut down the feed?" The other three men looked uncomfortably at the President.

The crowd was now in a complete frenzy. Beachum paused and briefly drank it in. "Friends, the road to November will not be easy. Much will be said and written about me and the citizens of this great state. But we must not waver in our fortitude to hold this vote and we must be prepared to honor its result. Should it be the will of the people that California go on a new path, separate from these once United States, then we shall take that path! Thank you and God Bless the great state of California."

The crowd roared with approval. The Vice-President held up the remote control and extinguished the feed. The room sat silent.

Champer looked at the three men around the table. "I want that fucker in handcuffs by morning and hanging from the flagpole of the White House by next week!"

16

July 10th, 2023

Somewhere over the Atlantic Ocean

"Calm down, Dick."

President Champer had ordered everyone out of the conference room and was now on a secure phone with Scott Burnside, who ran one of the largest right wing websites in the country and was a former executive at Fox News. "Easy for you to say, Scotty."

Burnside sighed. "I will admit, I didn't see something like this coming, but I think if we think it through, we can ultimately turn this to your benefit."

Champer paused and then leaned closer to the phone. "How so?"

Burnside paused as if in thought. "I'm not sure yet, Mr. President. But we have talked about how we continue the mission that we started nearly a decade ago and I think this could play an important part. I will admit that I'm not sure how yet, but I think it will."

Champer's eye brows rose. "You mean a third term?"

Burnside gave a short laugh. "Not necessarily that. It would be hard for us to go down a path like that." Burnside was clearly thinking as he spoke. He continued. "Maybe not impossible, as this sort of thing brings up the issue of war powers, but I was more eluding to the Partridge problem."

Champer sighed. "Scotty, I have told you that I like Pete and I don't want to replace him. I mean, we don't get the abortion law without him."

"I understand, sir. But we have also agreed that he does not agree with our approach to the border and to trade. And at the rate we are going, he is going to be the President in less than two years."

He paused. "For the country and for your legacy, I think at least considering replacing him with someone more aligned with the path you have set this country on is warranted."

"Who, Scotty?"

Burnside paused again. If Champer had been able to see him, he would have seen a big smile on his face. "I have a really exciting idea on that front, Mr. President."

17

July 10th, 2023

New York, New York

Matt Gibson stared at his Bloomberg screen. He was hopeful that Apple would hit $300 and then he'd buy more. It sat at $301.45, but was off $5 on the day against a weak tape.

Most of the televisions on the trading floor were tuned to CNBC and someone was giving a speech in front of a pretty large crowd. The sound was muted; although, the noise on the trading floor would have drowned out most of it anyway.

Gibson was hungry. While it was only 11:30, he had eaten breakfast at 6:30. He was trying to focus on Apple and on what he was going to send one of the minions on the trading floor to go fetch him for lunch.

Gibson continued to watch Apple, not interested in what was happening on the televisions. $301.41. He was prepared to buy 100,000 shares for an account if it broke $300 and then another 100,000 if it broke $298.

Maybe Mexican. $301.53 and then $301.44.

No, he had Mexican the day before. Maybe a sandwich from the good sandwich place as they called it. It was four blocks away and it was 92 degrees outside, but he wasn't going to get it, so what did he care.

$301.40 and then $265.12.

Gibson looked up from the screen. He said to no one in particular, "what the fuck? What the fuck?"

$229.43. Gibson then quickly typed in WEI on his Bloomberg to get a snapshot of the global indices. The S&P 500, which had been down about 1% on the session a few minutes before was now down 18%. The Dow was down 7,300 points at just above 39,000.

Greg Stevens yelled at Gibson, "Gibby!" and then pointed at the television.

Gibson stared at Stevens for a second and then looked up. Across the bottom the screen it read – California to vote to secede from the US.

18

September 2nd, 1987

Washington, District of Columbia

Ronald Reagan sipped his coffee. He had always been an early riser and had enjoyed the solitude of the first hour of the day when few were awake and no one tended to bother him.

That had all changed, of course. The past seven years had allowed little time for solitude, but as he neared the end of his run, as his wife had liked to say, he felt more comfortable imposing some rules on his staff.

Reagan's first rule "give me thirty minutes" had become the official directive of the President. I rise at 6 AM and you do not come into my office unless it's a national emergency until at least 6:30.

He turned the page of the front section of the Washington Post, which lay on his desk in the Oval Office. He preferred the LA Times, but it was not easy to get this early, even if you were the President of the United States and the leader of the free world.

Reagan pressed the intercom on his phone. It was 6:25.

"Yes, Mr. President?"

"Good morning, Judy."

Reagan could see her smile on the other end of the intercom. "Good morning, Mr. President."

"Judy, send in Howard."

"Yes, Mr. President."

Ten seconds later, Howard Baker walked through the Chief of Staff's door to the Oval.

"Good morning, Mr. President. We appear to be in violation of your first rule, sir."

Reagan smiled. "Nancy informed me that I cannot be in violation of my own rules."

Baker smiled back as he stood in front of Reagan's desk. "I doubt she said that, Mr. President."

Reagan frowned. "Are you calling me a liar, Howard?"

Baker shook his head. "Of course not, sir."

Reagan smiled. Baker was known as the "Great Conciliator" and Reagan was unsure whether his little joke had offended his new Chief of Staff. "At ease, Howard."

Baker smiled and winked at Reagan. They both shared a laugh.

"Howard, have a look at this." Reagan pointed to the paper.

Baker came around to the side of Reagan's desk and looked at the Post.

A full page ad read:

To the American People,

For decades, Japan and other nations have been taking advantage of the United States.

The world is laughing at American politicians as we protect ships we don't own, carrying oil we don't need, destined for allies who won't help.

Make Japan, Saudi Arabia and others pay for the protection we extend our allies. Let's help our farmers, our sick, our homeless by taking from some of the greatest profit machines ever created – machines created and matured by us. "Tax" these wealthy nations, not America. End our huge deficits, reduce our taxes, and let America's economy grow unencumbered by the cost of defending those who can easily afford to pay us for the defense of their freedom. Let's not let our great country be laughed at anymore."

Richard Champer

"Did he write that or the Soviets?" Baker took a seat opposite the President.

"Then it's not just me, Howard?" Reagan took a sip of his coffee.

Baker shook his head. "No sir, my former colleagues on the Senate Intelligence Committee are probably reading this, albeit not so early, and thinking the same thing."

"Is he going to run, Howard?"

Baker shrugged. "I don't think so, sir. No one has mentioned him as a potential candidate and to be honest, I'm not even sure if he's a democrat or a republican."

Reagan held up a part of the paper and waved it. "He's a damned isolationist. And he can't write worth a damn either."

Baker smiled. "Yes, sir."

Reagan sat back. "I can see it now. New York playboy Richard Champer running for President. His platform – Make America Great Again so it Doesn't get Laughed at Anymore."

Baker sat back. "He may want to shorten that to just the first part, but it's a start."

Reagan finished his coffee and looked at Baker. "It never ceases to amaze me the stupidity of the wealthy. The Soviets are looking for greedy, malleable rich people they can curry favor with because ..." Reagan paused for effect.

"Well, because you never know when you might catch a live one, Howard."

19

May 25th, 2016

New York, New York

Dimitri Restanov didn't like Champer's son. He reminded him of what the son of Dracula might look like if he were able to come out in the light day. But he was pliable and thus Restanov was sure that they would be able to use him for their purposes. "We have the emails. Not only some of hers, but many from members of the DNC."

"Why haven't you released them yet?"

Restanov smiled. "The Election is still almost five months away. Only in the last couple of weeks has it become clear that your father would win the nomination. Our view is that your father would be best served if we released the emails gradually with the heaviest concentration in October, so that it is fresh in voters' minds."

"Can you tell us what's in them?"

"Of course, but use it discreetly as there is an obvious danger to utilizing information that you are not supposed to have." Restanov was sure that Richard Champer Jr. was incapable of being discreet, but he figured a warning was still necessary.

"Of course," and then, "makes sense."

Restanov stared at the man. Richard Champer Sr. had inherited the necessary funds to launch his business career, but Restanov gave him some credit. Sure he had bankrupted several companies and screwed countless investors along the way, but he also had a knack for screwing over the little guy and that was very much the Russian way. His failures had also conveniently given Russia the opportunity to provide him with financial assistance.

He also liked that he put "Champ" on everything he owned. It exuded success even though beneath the surface he was just a glorified snake oil salesman. Again, the Russian way.

But his son – he had inherited everything, but his father's shrewdness. He was a snake oil salesman with no snakes and no oil. "We also have another separate plan."

"Are you going to hack the machines?"

Restanov smiled again. This one was stupid, but bold. "We are not quite there yet with the technology. But we have already undertaken an extensive social media plan designed to hurt her candidacy and help your father. While we do not expect it to have a big impact, we do think that it has the potential to move a couple of tight races in your favor, which may be all you need."

The President's son sagged a bit. "Damn, I was hoping you could hack those fuckers and lock this thing up for us."

Restanov sat back. "Next time, perhaps, next time."

20

September 2nd, 2028

San Mateo, California

The thermometer read 104.2. Manny had been struggling for six days and Lisa had finally been forced to take him to the emergency room.

Manny's small form was cuddled on her lap, sweat saturating his pajamas. Despite his high temperature, he was shivering; at times, uncontrollably.

"Miss Lopes?"

Lisa Lopes looked up from the shivering form of her young son. "Yes?"

Three minutes later, Lisa and Manny were in a small room just inside of pediatric emerge. A petite nurse, her hair tied in a tight bun lightly felt Manny's glands just below his chin. "How long has he been like this?"

"Ummm, almost a week," she said, using her well-practiced accent.

The nurse looked at her, eye brows raised. "He's had a temperature of over 102 for a week?"

Lisa nodded. "Almost a week."

The nurse turned back to Manny. "Why didn't you bring him in earlier?"

"Is he going to be okay?"

The nurse had laid Manny down on the bed he had been sitting on and was now listening to his chest. She then grabbed a clipboard she had placed next to Manny and jotted down some notes. She then turned back to Lisa. "Six days with a high fever can cause all kinds of problems."

Lisa nodded, fighting back sobs. She then let out a half-hearted, "I'm sorry."

The nurse stared at her for several seconds. She then turned to walk out of the room. "The doctor will be in shortly."

Lisa watched the nurse leave and the door close. She then heard the distinctive click of the bolt sliding. She crossed to the door. It was locked.

Lisa sat next to Manny. He seemed to have cooled a bit since she had taken his temperature an hour ago. He was asleep and not shivering like he had been when she brought him in. She stared at the door.

Five minutes later, the door opened and a greying man wearing a doctor's coat walked into the room. "Miss Lopes, I'm Doctor Jarvin." He gave her a comforting smile and extended his hand.

Lisa took the Doctor's hand, instantly feeling more at ease. "Lisa, please."

Dr. Jarvin looked at his clipboard. "Lisa, Manny is a pretty sick boy. We are going to need to take him for a few tests. Shouldn't take very long and we can hopefully get him right as rain."

Lisa gave a relieved smile. "Thank you, doctor."

A large orderly entered the room with a small gurney. He left the gurney in the doorway and moved over to Manny. With little effort, he lifted the small boy and carried and placed him comfortably on the gurney. Lisa moved to the gurney and kissed Emmanuel "Manny" Lopes on the forehead.

"Can I come with him?"

Doctor Jarvin stared at her for a moment, his reassuring smile still present. "It won't take very long. I think you'll be more comfortable here." Jarvin looked at the orderly and nodded.

"I'd like to be with him." Lisa pleaded.

Jarvin continued to smile. "He'll be fine. You stay here and we'll have him back to you in a jiff."

Jarvin nodded again to the orderly and said quietly, "let's go."

The orderly pushed the gurney out of the room and Doctor Jarvin backed out behind him, continuing to smile at Lisa as he shut the door. The lock fell into place a moment later.

Lisa sat back again on the bed that Manny had been on and stared at the door. She had tried everything for the past five years to avoid a moment like this. Born Luciana Marquez in El Salvador in 2006, she had come to the United States with her parents at the age of eight. The first few years in America were not without their challenges, but compared to what Luciana had remembered from her life in the outskirts of San Salvador, their small four-room apartment in East LA, which housed her and her three brothers, her parents and her father's brother, was a paradise.

Things began to change in 2017. ICE round-ups became more of an everyday occurrence and Luciana, who had by now become known as Lisa, would hear her parents talking quietly with her uncle about how people were disappearing – good people.

Although she wasn't supposed to, Lisa would often sneak a look from her doorway late at night, her three brothers sleeping behind her. There she would see her parents and uncle watching the happenings at the border. Images of small crying children and uniformed border agents. While Lisa did not understand it all, she understood enough to know that they were taking kids from their parents, which then became Lisa's daily worry.

At school every day, where most of the kids were like Lisa – Carmela was now Karen, Guillermo was now Billy – Lisa would often stare out the window at the passing cars, waiting for the black SUVs that were synonymous with ICE raids.

For a few years, her fears proved unwarranted. Lisa and her family seemed to fly under the radar as did many of the families close to them in their neighborhood. Even when the Great Wall of Champer, as it had come to be known, had started to go up, their little enclave was seemingly ignored. And then Governor Beachum had made his announcement – everything had changed after that.

The door to the room opened. Lisa knew before that what was coming. She had seen too many things over the past few years, including the disappearance of two of her brothers and Manny's father, Jefe "Jeff" Lopez "Lopes".

Two ICE officers walked in. Lisa buried her head in her hands. What would they do with Manny?

21

June 29th, 2034

Los Angeles, California

"So how much do you know?" Larry continued to point the two guns at Dougherty, Richards and Kennex, while talking to Karen.

"We know you are not Larry Stabler," Kennex replied.

Larry turned to him. "How?"

Kennex stared at him. "Personal files. I have access to them and we do routine checks and yours came up a bit, ummm, odd."

"Who's we?"

Kennex looked at Karen, who nodded. "FOB."

Larry didn't flinch. Anyone who watched the news, even if it was virtually all state run media and thus to be taken with a grain of salt, was familiar with the "evils" of the Friends Of Beachum movement. "So this is FOB?"

Karen interjected. "A small piece of it, but a very important piece." She paused. "The tip of the spear."

Larry studied her for a moment. "So Jack goes through personal files and he finds what?"

Ken Dougherty now interrupted. "Jack's not the only one. We go through files every day in a lot of different places, looking for those who might be, ummm, supportive of the cause."

Larry looked at Dougherty, who had mustard on his chin. "What do you look for?"

Kennex now spoke. "Backstories that don't check out. I have to admit that whoever wrote the story of Larry Stabler did an amazing job of filling in the gaps. I'm not sure we wouldn't have, ummm, dropped the file, if it weren't for a tell."

Larry looked at Kennex. "A tell?"

Karen now weighed in. "Your story was almost too good – Larry Stabler, never married, no kids, raised in Sacramento, parents died when he was twenty in a car crash. Never returned a library book late, in fact, never took out a library book as far as we could tell. Never served, never voted, paid all his bills. Never been in trouble. Never really anything at all."

Dougherty then spoke. "I've been doing this long enough to know that everyone leaves a digital trail of some sort. Twitter, Facebook, Oculus, those are the obvious ones, but I can believe that someone can eschew all social media in the name of staying off the grid. But everything we do these days is tracked, Larry. This has obviously gotten even

95

worse the past ten-years with mandatory registration and all the checkpoints we have to pass through every day. We are constantly being logged and thus our footprint grows and grows. You, Larry, have just about the lightest step I have ever seen. It was too perfect, which made us dig deeper."

"And what did you find?"

Karen now spoke. "Nothing. Before you start firing bullets, I am going to be completely up front with you, Larry. We had no idea who you were, but based on Jack's assessment and Jack is pretty fuckin' good at this, we were pretty sure you were worth trying to recruit. He's been watching you for a while and was nearly 100% you were former military and given the extensive cover up of your identity, which could have only been pulled off by real pros, and it was worth, ummm, an attempt."

Larry looked at Kennex. There was a time he would have known he was being watched, but apparently Kennex had surveilled him for some time without him having any clue. He was getting old and rusty. "So you staged the incident the other night?"

Karen now smiled at him. "Yes, we have found the best way to recruit is to create a situation such as the one the other night. It allows us to not only see if you can be recruited, but also to see the skills that you have."

Larry stared at her. "That's a pretty fuckin' dangerous way to do things. How could you be sure I wouldn't shoot you?"

Richards now spoke. "Because the gun in your right hand is full of blanks."

Larry looked down at the Glock. He then fired it at Richards. A loud roar filled the room. Richards raised his hands to his face as if to ward off the bullet, but he was un-wounded.

After several beats of silence, Kennex started laughing at the same time he put his fingers in his ears turning them to try and clear the noise. "That was fucking brilliant."

Larry lowered the Glock and shifted the Sig to his right hand and backed away a step to give him more of a sweep of the room. "So you broke into my apartment, found the gun and made sure I wasn't going to shoot anyone." He said this as a statement rather than a question.

Karen nodded. "Something like that."

"Did I pass your test?"

Karen now smiled. "I think you know you did. Your handling of the situation was about all we could have hoped for and more."

"And what about the guy whose head I bashed in?"

Karen squinted. "A necessary cost of doing business. He'll recover, albeit he may need some work on his nose before he breathes quite right again."

"Can I ask you a question, Larry?"

Larry turned to look at Dougherty. He then nodded.

"How did you piece this together? I mean, you told us your golden rules and all, but aside from some coincidences and your gut, how'd you figure we were setting you up?"

Larry stared at Dougherty and then looked at the others. "Probably the same way you found me. The other night seemed a bit too perfect. And then my observations of my place and your place didn't seem quite right – again, too perfect."

Dougherty nodded. Karen then spoke. "Can I ask you another question? Actually two."

Larry looked at her. He then nodded.

"Who are you really, Larry and could you lower the gun?"

22

July 18th, 2023

Albany, New York

CNN anchor Lauren Castor stared at the Governor. It was the moment of truth in the interview. She had already gotten from her the general reaction to what Beachum had done, but now she had come to what those in the industry liked to refer to as "the Pulitzer moment." She shifted in her chair and smiled at Governor Cossimo. "Governor, what will New York do?"

Cossimo stared back at Castor lost in thought. Three days earlier, she had met with Messimer, Deacon, Silver and Sully. They had gone round and round on Beachum's announcement, what was likely to happen to him, whether or not California would ever get to a vote and ultimately, what New York should do.

They all agreed that Beachum and California stood a much better chance of "surviving" the next four months if other states stood with them. And by other states, the only one that really mattered was New York, as together, they represented nearly a quarter of the country's GDP, controlled two of the largest ports in the country and in the case of New York, controlled most of the financial machinations of the country.

Cossimo had encouraged them to be honest and not tell her what she wanted to hear. Stacey Silver had pointed out that if they did this, they would have a problem with Staten Island and upstate. Support in New York City and downstate would be very strong and the vote, if they got that far, would almost certainly be in favor of secession, but they would have a divided state.

George Deacon had thought that the mere act of support without even discussing or scheduling a vote might be enough to diffuse the situation. Even an Administration as recalcitrant as this one would probably back off and agree to talks when faced with the "defection" of two of the three largest states in the Union.

Not surprisingly, Sully had steadfastly disagreed with Deacon – she did not refer to them as the Toxic Twins for nothing after her favorite band when growing up – Aerosmith. He was adamant that Champer and his goon squad as Sully liked to call them, were just as likely to start dropping bombs on New York and California and fueled by their propagandists at Fox News and a feckless Congress – get away with it.

While the meeting never gave way to shouts, all sides were fairly entrenched in their views. Cossimo thanked them without signaling to them what she would do either way and urged them all to be discreet with discussing the meeting, even though she trusted them implicitly.

Cossimo looked at Castor. "Lauren, New York fully supports its friends in California."

Castor tried not to display any emotion. Holy shit, holy shit, holy shit. "And what does that mean exactly?"

Cossimo focused on the anchor. "I believe that what Governor Beachum said the other day is 100% correct. We have all stood by as this country has become deeply divided and we have watched as the laws and regulations have been changed, even though a distinctive majority of this country does not want this to happen. We have also done this under the umbrella of a political system, which no longer guarantees that the will of the majority will be heard; and, quite to the contrary, in fact, seems to now guarantee that those in power will remain in power, despite the will of the majority."

"So you will hold a vote as well?"

Cossimo smiled. "We are not there yet, but I would not rule it out. We support California's right to do what is doing and call upon our government to sit down, not only with California, but also with other states that do not see eye to eye with the general direction of things over these past seven years." She paused. "The bottom line is that things must change and they must change immediately. Our approach to immigration must change. Our approach to the environment must change. Our approach to a woman's right to choose must change, including the immediate suspension of this terrible Federal bill that cannot possibly withstand Supreme Court review regardless of how tainted the Court has become."

"Or else?"

Cossimo squinted again and then paused for two beats. "Let me put it to you this way, Lauren. We all want to make America great again, we just have a different view on what this means."

23

November 9, 2013

Moscow, Russia

Richard Champer walked out of the bathroom, wearing only a robe. He observed the large Ritz Carlton presidential suite and smiled to himself. While it did not have all of the accoutrements of the West, Moscow had come a long way in 25-years.

Champer looked again at the note from the Russian president. He was disappointed that Popov would not be meeting him at the Pageant, but the connection he had built with Agas Agalarov, the wealthiest man in Russia, over the past half year could be hugely valuable. The Russians had helped him immensely in the 1990's when he had been in financial distress – let's see how they can help me when my finances are in better shape.

Champer prepared to dress for dinner. He would be meeting Agalarov and some of his aides, as well as some of the ladies from the Miss Universe Pageant. To think he had been paid $20 million to bring the Pageant to Moscow and he was rewarded with wealthy connections and dinner with a bevy of young beauties. Life was indeed good.

His clothes had been laid out on the bed and Champer prepared to remove his robe. Before he could, there was a knock on the door.

He walked to the door and answered it.

"Mr. Champer?" Two woman stood at the door. Both wore grey trench coats. One had short blonde hair and the other had long red hair. They both looked to be about 20-years of age. Champer stared at them; he was certain they were the two most beautiful women he had ever met in his life, which was saying something. The blonde spoke with a thick Russian accent, while the red head simply stared seductively at Champer.

Champer smiled. "Richard Champer at your service."

The two walked into his room without being invited. Again, the blonde spoke. "Mr. Agalarov asked us to escort you to dinner."

Champer motioned to his robe. "I'm sorry ladies, I have not had a chance to get dressed yet."

The red head shut the door. "That's okay, neither have we." They both removed their coats, they wore nothing underneath. Thirty seconds later, they had moved to the bedroom.

From above the mantle in the bedroom, a camera zoomed in.

24

July 16, 2018

Helsinki, Finland

"You understand the consequences?"

The two translators nodded and moved to the right side of the large room near the door. Russian President Alexei Popov removed a small iPod from his breast pocket and set it on the table, turning it on as he did so. Russian music began to play.

Champer smiled. He then said in a loud whisper, "you are a crafty one, my friend."

Popov nodded. He said in almost flawless English, "we have done great things, you and I, and we shall continue to do great things."

"You saw how I treated the Europeans? Or should I say mistreated the Europeans? NATO has served its purpose and the United States will no longer throw good money after bad defending those that treat it like a cash machine."

Popov stared back at him. "Let us discuss what we talked about before the election."

Champer had been waiting for this moment. He had promised Popov an awful lot, or at least his people had, and he had wondered when the bills might come due. "Mr. President, I am not sure what you mean?"

Popov gave a small smile. He had suspected that Champer would force him to ask as opposed to volunteer anything himself. He decided a small threat would be a good opening salvo. "As you know, Mr. President, we have accumulated, ummm," he paused purposely acting as if he could not find the words, "information over the past thirty-years on a variety of people in your country."

He paused again this time to look at the two translators who stood facing the wall. "This information is kept under very close guard in my country because of the damage it could do to our friends in America."

Champer smiled. "I understand completely, Alexei. Who would want these people to get hurt?"

Popov nodded. "Exactly, Mr. President. We would not want that to happen. And, of course, then there are the loans that were made more than a decade ago."

While Popov did not add "to your organization", Champer appeared to get the reference. "Loans that I believe have been repaid, Alexei."

Popov smiled. "Of course, Mr. President."

Champer leaned in. "Alexei, I get the sense that the American people have very little tolerance left for sacrificing American lives in some faraway land. It worries me really because we have such a mighty army that probably needs to fight from time to time to stay fresh."

Popov nodded. "We both have very powerful armies, do we not?"

"Oh, of course we do. It's just that ours is the strongest and it has really gotten much stronger since I became President. All my generals tell me that, so I guess it must be true."

Popov stared at Champer for two beats. "So how do we balance, Mr. President, the needs of Russia and the needs of the United States and at the same time make sure that all of this valuable information stays hidden?"

Champer smiled. "As I was saying, Alexei. I don't think the American people want to see their young boys killed in some war in Eastern Europe. We have lost too many over the years and what is the thanks we get? They laugh at us and say how stupid we are for letting them take advantage of us."

Popov nodded. "This is good to hear, Mr. President."

Champer leaned in again. "But Alexei, the timing must be right. We have mid-term elections coming up and soon I will be running again. We cannot have you running roughshod all over Europe in the middle of a Presidential campaign or God forbid with the Democrats in charge of Congress."

Popov smiled for the first time in their meeting. "Mr. President, I think we understand each other very well."

25

September 4th, 2023

Sacramento, California

Larry awoke from his usual light slumber. For a moment he was unsure of where he was, but then he felt something pressed against his right leg. He focused his thoughts and picked out the deep breaths of Beth, who slept behind him and further down the bed, buried under the covers, the quiet whispering of Cody, who was "spooned" against Larry's leg. The clock read 5:07 – he had to get up.

Larry deftly slid his leg up with the Spooner still attached. He left the small boy sleeping on Larry's pillow and he trod off to the bathroom.

After showering, Larry stood in front of the mirror. He had lost about 50-pounds of muscle over the years and was now much slighter of build. There was nary an ounce of fat on his tight, muscled frame, but he was no longer "the Red Bear" as he had been called back in the service.

After looking for any obvious signs of aging, a strange habit Larry had developed over the years, he grabbed his suit, which he had hung on the inside of the bathroom door the night before, and quickly dressed.

Before going downstairs, Larry checked on the baby, who was now almost five years old. Satisfied that no one had stolen him while Larry had slept, he quietly shut his door and made his way downstairs to the kitchen.

Larry unlocked a cabinet door at the bottom of the island and removed his Glock G17. He also kept one locked in the bedroom in case his past ever came calling, but this was his carry weapon. He checked the clip and then holstered the gun in his vest.

Within 10-minutes, Larry was behind the wheel of his 2017 Jeep Cherokee and cruising down "the five" at 75 miles per hour.

As he stared out at the road and the few cars that were out there with him, his mind wandered to the upcoming day. He had reviewed the team files the night before, even though he was well aware of not only every man on his detail, but who was assigned to the detail from day to day. Nonetheless, he had learned over the years that one could never be too thorough and something he had not discovered or thought of before might rear its ugly head at the most inopportune time.

Larry's gut told him that today would be a tough day. He had made sure the team was on heightened alert for the past two months, but the news reports from the night before suggested that today could be especially contentious.

President Champer had been giving what could only be described as a fiery campaign speech in Kentucky the night before. Even though the Constitution barred him from a third term, he did not seem like a man who was no longer running for office and the pundits had begun to take notice.

Making matters worse, news reports were full of the wall to wall coverage of the Russian invasion of Poland and Finland, not to mention the massive damage done to Champ Tower in Manhattan at the hands of an angry mob.

Champer had found a way to not only blame California for the Russian invasion, but he also seemed to somehow find justification in what they had done. At one point, the President had even gone as far to intimate that that Russian President had told them that Russia was defending itself and that somehow Champer had no reason to doubt Popov's word.

Yeah, something told Larry that this was going to be a tough day.

26

November 8th, 2016

Washington, District of Columbia

Dimitri smiled. The night was going according to plan. Wisconsin had just been called for Champer – a huge upset as the pundits had put it in the Likely Democrat column.

He thought back to the night of October 21st, 2015. He had been arguing with Sergei about Champer and whether he could pull off the impossible. Operation Orangutan, which Dimitri had personally named it, had been launched soon after he had announced – how do we get this man elected?

Hillary Clinton was clearly going to be the Democratic candidate and she was vulnerable. Her husband had been a popular President, but also one shrouded in scandal. The Russians specialized in scandals and the propaganda of taking seemingly explainable and innocuous situations and making them seem sketchy.

On the 21st, he and Sergei had sat in a bar in Georgetown. While Sergei spoke with a slight accent, no one took notice of a Russian and his "American" colleague debating politics. As they went back and forth on Orangutan, the baseball game unfolded on the screens around the bar.

Dimitri had spent most of his adult life in America. He loved the country, even though he despised most of its inhabitants and the hubris, which they displayed on a daily basis. Orangutan would change that. Dimitri was almost certain of it. He had grown to love baseball, even though it was foreign to most in his mother Russia.

He turned to Sergei Metzokov as the crowd in the bar let out a collective cheer. "You see, Sergei? It can be done." As he said this, Dimitri pointed to the screen.

Metzokov, who had not been in the US for very long and thus had little interest in baseball, turned to the screen. "What has happened?"

"Hell has frozen over, my friend. The Cubs of Chicago have won the World Series. Now indeed, anything is possible."

Dimitri returned to the television screen. Michigan was trending strongly in favor of Champer. His math, which was based on complex algorithms developed by their "algo team" told him that Wisconsin coupled with Michigan all but assured that Champer would be President.

He sat back and sipped his glass of vodka. This was far too easy, he thought to himself. At a cost of less than $20 million, they had pushed the US election to Champer. While this represented only the first stage of Orangutan, it was obviously the most important. With "the Orangutan's son" already within their clutches and several members of his team, the next four and probably eight years would bring huge changes for the future of Mother Russia.

"CNN is ready to project that Michigan and its 16 electoral will go to Richard Champer in what can only be called an enormous upset."

Dimitri smiled – so easy.

27

February 4th, 2009

Kabul, Afghanistan

"Good luck, Larry."

Larry looked over his shoulder at Colonel Davies and nodded. He then opened the door off his office and walked into a small side room.

Two men sat at a table. One wore grey shorts and a black White Stripes tee-shirt, while the other was dressed in white pants and a short-sleeved blue button down. They both looked to be in their early 30s and Larry instantly got the sense that among other things -they were killers.

"Sergeant Nash, please sit."

Larry nodded and sat at a chair across from the two men. "I'm Malcolm and this is Craig." The White Stripes man spoke, smiling the whole time. Larry noted that there were no last names provided.

Larry nodded to the man identified as Craig and then stared back at Malcolm. After a brief pause. "Larry, I'm not going to bullshit you as we have reviewed your record, including what you did tonight and I am fairly confident that there is no need for bullshit." He paused and then said, "is that fair?"

Larry stared at Malcolm and then nodded.

Malcolm smiled and looked at Craig. "He doesn't say an awful lot." Craig said nothing, but squinted at Larry.

Larry shrugged and then spoke. "Neither does he."

Malcolm smiled again. "Fair enough. We'd like to talk to you about an opportunity."

Malcolm paused and Larry felt they were expecting him to respond. He took the bait. "What sort of opportunity?"

Craig now spoke for the first time. "We think that you have a certain set of skills that may be useful to some of the things we are trying to accomplish."

"Like Liam Neeson?"

Malcolm and Craig looked at each other and Malcolm then laughed. "Yes, like Liam effen Neeson." He then did an impersonation of Neeson, which wasn't half bad. "I have are a very particular set of skills. Skills I have acquired over a very long career. Skills that make me a nightmare for people like you. If you let my daughter go now that'll be the end of it."

Malcolm then laughed again. Larry allowed himself a small smile. While he rightly feared the two men across the table, there was something disarming

116

about Malcolm that was hard not to like. He didn't doubt that one would regret getting on Malcolm's bad side, but Larry felt he could appreciate being on his good side.

Larry decided a direct assault was now warranted. "What does the CIA want with my skills?"

Malcolm stopped laughing and he and Craig once again looked at one another. After a moment, Craig nodded and Malcolm spoke. "Not to be overly dramatic, Larry, but this world is full of some very dangerous people. Now, we are not naïve and we realize that every time someone takes out a dangerous person that they can be replaced with another dangerous person and it's inevitably a merry-go-round, but that doesn't mean that we shouldn't make every effort to keep the merry-go-round spinning."

Larry stared back at him and then looked at Craig. "And you guys keep the merry-go-round spinning?"

Malcolm smiled. "In a matter of speaking. We operate outside certain lines to make sure that things that need to get done, get done."

Larry sat back in his chair. "How would this work?"

Malcolm looked at Craig, who now spoke. "You'd be honorably discharged and join our team. We'd give you a bit of training in wet ops and some of the other things we do and you'd then be on the books with the Central Intelligence Agency. We've already done a thorough background on you, so we don't need to jump through that usual hoop, so soup-to-nuts, we are probably up and running in six weeks."

Larry stared back at Craig. He had joined the military after his junior year at UCLA. It had been an unusual route as Larry was only 10 credits from graduating and most didn't enlist when they were set to get a college degree. But Larry had thought about it for a while and he had decided that if he was ever going to matter to this world, his window was rapidly closing.

He had just broken up with his girlfriend of two years, Beth Jennings, and while his gut told him that even though the break-up had been a bad one, Beth might still be the one. But the break-up had "opened the window" so to speak and Larry had decided to step through it. That said – he did not view the military as a career, but rather a stop along the way.

He had already given it two-years and he realized that while he did indeed have "a certain set of skills", he did not plan to do this forever.

"How long?"

Malcolm and Craig again looked at each other. While Larry's question was vague, they both seemed to understand. Malcolm shrugged. "As long as you want. Unless you decide to make this a career." He paused. "Don't believe the bullshit that once you are in the CIA, you are in it for life."

Craig smiled. It was not a pretty sight and Larry silently hoped not to see it again. "It's not like you read in books, Larry. No one is going to visit you in the middle of the night when you decide you've had enough and cut your throat." He made a subtle throat slashing gesture – the sinister smile remained.

Larry looked at Malcolm. He preferred talking to him; although he tried not to show it. "And if I say no?"

"Don't say no, Larry." The room was silent for a moment and then Malcolm started laughing again. "I'm just fucking with you, Larry." He snorted, clearly happy with his joke. He then paused. "If you decide to take the blue pill, you walk back through that door." He pointed at the door leading back to Colonel Davies office. "But if you decide to take the red pill, he paused again, "well then, we show you the matrix."

For the first time, Larry gave a genuine smile as Malcolm laughed again at his own reference. After a pause, "okay, give me the red pill."

28

August 11th, 2019

Denver, Colorado

Charlie "Chuck" Hamilton stared across the breakfast table at his wife. "I agree, Les. We owe it to Ricky and Jackie and the girls."

Leslie Hamilton smiled through tears at her husband of 24-years. She realized at that moment that they would be parents for the first time after trying for the better part of a decade to no avail.

"So, are we ready for this?"

Chuck smiled. "Let's go talk to them."

The two rose from the table and walked through their kitchen into the family room. Three girls, ages sixteen, eleven and four sat on a large couch.

Chuck and Leslie sat across from them on a small loveseat. Chuck spoke first. "Naomi, Rachel, Leah, Leslie and I wanted to talk to you about something."

The three girls sat quietly. Naomi looked at her younger sisters and then back at Chuck and Leslie. "Mr. and Mrs. Hamilton, we know we were pretty loud last night after lights out and ..."

Chuck held up his hand. "Sweetie, I know I was in the military and I know I have some odd rules that come from those days, but it's not about that." He paused to build up his courage. "We wanted to talk to you about the future."

Leslie now spoke. "It's been almost a year and a half and we have loved looking after the three of you. This was an impossibly difficult situation for the three of you and you are amazing girls, but it's time now to talk about the future."

Naomi looked again at her sisters and then spoke. "You mean it's time for us to go, don't you?"

Chuck smiled and shook his head. "The opposite honey, we want you to live with us permanently." He paused again to build some courage. "Leslie and I would like to adopt the three of you."

Rachel now spoke. "Become our mom and dad?"

Leslie smiled. "In a way, sweetie. We can never replace your mom and dad. They were wonderful people and dear, dear friends of ours ..."

"But we owe it to them and we owe it to you to move on and make sure that the three of you live the wonderfully rewarding lives your parents would have wanted you to have ..."

"And Chuck and I would like to be a part of that if you will have us."

Naomi Lopez stared at the only two people left alive she had known all of her life. Her parents had fled Nicaragua in the late 1990's, eventually making their way to America. Her father, Enrique "Ricky" Lopez had always dreamed of living in the mountains and he and Marie had eventually settled in a suburb of Denver.

Ricky was a master with his hands and with a car engine and even though his illegal status made it difficult to find work on the books, he was able to build a business fixing cars and other stuff. Eventually, he became well known for his skills and relatively low cost and the business grew from there.

Ricky and Marie's next door neighbors were the Hamiltons. Even though Ricky and Marie struggled with the language, the four had become fast friends. After leaving the army, Chuck had struggled to find steady work and the two survived mostly on Leslie's nursing salary. Chuck, who was also pretty handy, began to work with Ricky and the two eventually opened up an auto repair shop in Chuck's name.

Five years later, the two couples had become so close that when the Hamiltons wanted to move to a swankier neighborhood, the Lopez's moved to the house next door. A year after that, Naomi was born.

Chuck and Leslie had struggled for years to have kids of their own. Leslie had miscarried three times and eventually the thought of getting pregnant again and "failing" was too great for her to bear.

The Lopez's had helped them get through "the dark years" as Leslie called them. She wasn't sure they would have gotten through it without them.

The Hamiltons had reluctantly settled into their lives as childless when the world suddenly changed on October 14th, 2017.

Auto repair was a challenging business. Most customers left satisfied and Chuck, Ricky and their team of six other mechanics at Chuck's Auto were known for doing really good work. But customers could also be fickle and Ricky had caught a repair job on a 2013 BMW X5, which had just come off warranty.

The owner of the X5, a man named Arthur Laskey, was ticked off that BMW would not cover the repair on the engine, which Ricky quoted at $6,500 plus tax.

Two days later, Ricky phoned Laskey, who returned to the shop. The situation quickly deteriorated with Laskey alternatively claiming that he had not authorized the work and that the quoted price had included tax.

Ricky had built his career on honest work. That said – he wasn't itching for a fight and agreed to quote the job at $6,500 including tax, which Laskey had reluctantly paid by credit card.

A day later, the credit card company called to inform them that the charge was under dispute.

Chuck, who handled all the paperwork, forwarded the details of the job to the Visa representative. These things happened from time to time and they generally resolved in their favor, so Chuck made a note to circle back in a few days and moved on to other work.

A day later – October the 14th – ICE showed up. Eight Immigration and Customs Enforcement officers raided Chuck's Auto. A day later, they picked up Marie.

Because the three girls were born in the United States and American citizens, they had been left in limbo. Chuck and Leslie immediately took them in and hired immigration lawyers to defend Ricky and Marie.

Six weeks later, Enrique and Marie Lopez were deported to Nicaragua. They had not been there in 22-years.

Four weeks after that, Ricky and Marie attempted to journey back to the United States. They made it as far Veracruz, Mexico where they were to board a boat that would attempt entry into the US along the Texas coast.

Two days later, their bodies would wash onshore. Both had been shot once in the back of the head.

The Hamiltons had decided to be up front with the Lopez girls about what had happened. Leah was thankfully too young to understand, but Rachel and especially Naomi had been devastated. For months, Naomi went into a shell, her idyllic life with loving parents suddenly cast into chaos because of a disgruntled customer.

After about six months of mourning, Naomi had a vivid dream. In it, her father stood on the deck of a boat, his hands bound behind his back.

Rather than looking panicked, he was perfectly calm. He told Naomi to come stand next to him and he told her to lift herself out of her shell because her sisters needed her. He then said and she remembered his words exactly, "turn your despair into resolve."

She awoke and from that moment forward, her view on life and that of her sisters was changed. No longer would she despair about the injustice done to her parents. Rather, she had resolved to live the life they had tried to build for her.

And while she could not recall her father telling her this in the dream, she felt it deeply inside – eventually, she would collect the debt.

Naomi continued to stare at the Hamiltons. "Uncle Chuck, Aunt Leslie, we would like that very much."

29

July 17th, 2023

New York, New York

Mitch Peters looked at former White House Press Secretary Steve Sellers. "This President has shown time and time again, Steve, that he will not be pushed around and I don't think this will be any different."

"I agree, Mitch. This President should not treat California with kid gloves for what it's trying to do, but should be prepared to put every option on the table."

"And by every option you mean the military option and I agree." Peters now looed directly into the camera. "Look, I don't like the idea of US solders having to be deployed on US soil any more than any of our viewers do. But Mr. President, you cannot take the military option off the table because what California is trying to do is nothing short of an act of treason."

The two continued to go back and forth on the different reasons the US should be prepared to invade California.

Peters smiled to the camera. "That's all we have time for tonight folks. I'd like to thank my guest tonight, Steve Sellers, former White House Press

Secretary under President Champer for sharing his views this evening. You've been watching Fox News and Peters on Politics. Until next time."

Scott Burnside clicked off his television. He was sure that Champer would be watching and he would get the message – a firm stand was necessary.

Burnside's phone rang. It would be Mitch Peters trying to find out how he had done. Burnside decided to let it ring through to voicemail.

30

July 18th, 2023

Washington, District of Columbia

President Richard Champer sat at his large desk in the Oval Office. He was proud to note to anyone who came in that his desk was bigger than that of any other President of the United States. He purposely had his chair designed to sit him at least six inches higher than the guest chair across from the desk. Champer stood almost six-feet three-inches and with his 250+ pound frame, he already cut an imposing figure, despite being nearly 80-years old. Seated high up behind his large desk, the imposition was further enhanced.

Across from the desk and against the wall were a bank of 12-televisions that Champer had insisted be installed. Most were tuned to either Fox News or CNN, with a couple tuned to MSNBC and CNBC.

President Champer tried to give his best tough guy squint to his Chief of Staff. "Dammit, Cal, why the fuck not?"

Retired three-star General Calvin "Cal" Doggett stared back at Champer. Doggett was the fourth man to occupy the COS seat and the second retired general. Champer "liked his generals" and Doggett had reluctantly accepted the role the year before, knowing that it had not gone particularly well for any of his predecessors. He neither liked nor respected Champer, but he did appreciate that the man was malleable if one was patient and was willing to take the repeated body blows that Champer liked to land both face-to-face and through his Twitter account.

"As we discussed, sir - the senior staff believes the best course of action is to continue the PR campaign, as you have done so effectively over these past few weeks."

Champer shook his head. "We need to do more than that – what about the military option?"

Doggett paused. He knew he had to lead the dog by the leash, but the dog had to be convinced that the path he was following was his own path and not the path that his master intended all along.

"We are working on the military option. Operation United Coast has several splash teams working on it as we speak with some of the best military planners we have working through tactics, logistics, time tables and scenarios."

Doggett had purposely made his statement sound complex, making sure to use words that portrayed strength. He knew how to hold the leash.

Champer sat back. "Operation United Coast. I do like that. Take me through what we have so far."

Doggett paused again. He had to be careful at this point and he knew it. His duty to country still mattered a lot to him and simply pleasing his boss with some jingoistic lingo could muddy the waters down the road. He also knew that his boss had a very big mouth and there was the risk that he could leak information either on purpose or by accident that would throttle the operation before it got off the ground.

"As I said, we have our best minds working on different aspects of the plan, but as you can imagine, the situation is fluid at this point. We are still roughly 90-days from the vote and our view remains that we should allow the vote to happen with no interference from us, at least of a physical nature."

"Yes, yes, okay. But take me through the bones of the plan. How do you see it playing out?"

"Yes, sir. The basics of the plan will be that in the event of a "yes" vote; that is, California votes to secede, we use both Beale and Edwards as staging areas. Within 12-hours of the vote, we can have 50,000 troops on the ground and we would set up choke points all around Los Angeles, San Diego, San Francisco and, of course, Sacramento. We would use Camp Parks to mobilize and supply Frisco and Loma as a staging area for San Diego."

Champer gave a content smile. "Overwhelming force then."

"Yes, sir. We estimate that within 24-hours of initial deployment we will control all traffic into and out of California and we would have Beachum and his senior staff in custody. Ideally without a single shot fired. You would declare martial law, at least until we have things settled down."

Champer liked the sound of martial law. "And if there's resistance, where does it come from?"

"Our intel suggests to us that Beachum's security detail is pretty loyal to him. Several are ex-military with his Head of Security one really tough hombre. They might not go quietly, even if Beachum instructs them to."

Champer nodded. "And the general public?"

Doggett paused. Here is where he struggled a bit with country versus duty. "Well, sir, the populace is going to be pretty charged up about the result of the vote. They've bristled under some of the things that have been done over the past seven years ..."

"... fuckin' liberal pansies. Don't they know we have every right to do what we've done? I was elected and don't believe what you fucking read about how the vote went – I was elected by a majority of this fucking country and I am not going to let some liberal fucking enclave of immigrants and faggots tell me how to fucking govern!"

"Yes sir. But nonetheless, we do think there is a risk that civilians fight back and thus we will be prepared with tear gas and rubber bullets."

"Rubber bullets? Fuck that. This is a mutiny and you do not put down a mutiny with rubber bullets and tear gas."

Doggett paused. Loosen the leash a bit. "Yes, sir. We would initially meet resistance with rubber bullets and gas; however, we would be prepared to engage with conventional weapons if necessary."

Champer paused and then nodded. "Very good, general." Champer sat back. Just then, the door to his right opened.

"Sir, I think you should listen to this." Vice-President, Peter Partridge, who Champer had ordered to stay at the White House while this was unfolding, grabbed the remote from the President's desk and unmuted CNN.

New York Governor Brenda Cossimo, who Champer simply referred to as "the cunt" was being interviewed.

"Governor, what will New York do?" It was Lauren Castor asking the question – Champer had a thing for Castor. He imagined at if he had run into her a few years back, he might be a part of the many stories he liked to share with his close friends.

"Lauren, New York fully supports its friends in California."

"And what does that mean exactly?" Castor replied with a somewhat surprised look.

"I believe that what Governor Beachum said the other day is 100% correct. We have all stood by as this country has become deeply divided and we have watched as the laws and regulations have been changed, even though a distinctive majority of this country does not want this to happen …"

Champer slammed the desk. "Turn that shit off!"

Partridge muted the television.

"I said off, Pete. Not fucking muted. Off!"

Partridge looked down and fumbled with the remote for a few seconds. Ultimately, he turned off all the screens as he could not just manage to turn off just CNN. Doggett shifted uncomfortably in his chair.

Champer looked at him and then at Partridge. He said calmly, "I want an invasion plan on my desk by morning."

End Part 1

31

June 29ᵗʰ, 2034

Los Angeles, California

Larry lowered the Sig. He pulled back the chair that he had been sitting in and sat down. "You can tell the guy in the other room to lower his gun and come out here."

Kennex smiled. "Cory, why don't you join us?"

From the doorway behind Kennex and Karen emerged what Larry would describe as a mass of pure muscle. He was dressed in black pants and a dark blue tee-shirt. He neither smiled nor acknowledged Larry. The gun he had held was no longer visible. The man was roughly six feet tall and had sandy brown hair. He appeared to Larry to be in his early 30s, making him the youngest man in the room by at least a decade and roughly Karen's age.

"Larry this is Cory Nelson. Cory, this is Larry, ummm, this is Larry Stabler."

Larry squinted at Nelson and then nodded. Nelson continued to stand behind Kennex and Karen, but he too now nodded to Larry.

Larry now looked back at Karen. "I don't think I'm ready yet to tell you who I am."

Karen nodded. "That's fair, but you're here and you are no longer pointing a gun at us, so I'd call that progress."

Kennex now spoke. "Okay, you are not ready to share with us, Larry and that's fine. Can we share with you?"

Larry knew what he meant by this. Telling him they were FOB was already a big step as Larry could get a healthy reward for turning them in. However, sharing FOB battle plans was an entirely different kettle of fish.

Larry nodded. "I've lived a quiet life the past few years as you have so effectively laid out. Let's say I am prepared for it to be less quiet."

Karen smiled. Between the other night and the past few minutes, she was quickly enamored with Larry Stabler or whatever his name really was. He had striking blue eyes and a slash of red hair that made for a compelling combination. His eyes portrayed sadness to be sure and the flecks of grey and battle lines on his face suggested he may be old enough to be her father, but there was something about him that she found very attractive.

Karen looked at Richards, "Phil, why don't you fill Larry in?"

Richards nodded. "We have pretty solid intel that Champer is coming to California, Larry."

Larry stared at him and then replied, "all due respect, but that's not much intel."

Richards smiled. "We have pretty solid intel that he's coming here and that part of his itinerary includes a stop at the Long Beach docks."

Larry sat back in his chair. So here it was. "I see."

Karen now spoke. "Larry, we have plan to start a counter-offensive of sorts, but the tip of the spear is taking out Champer. We see the docks as the best chance for this with Jack already stationed there. As you can appreciate, he's not enough, which is where you come in."

Larry looked at Kennex and then back at Karen. "All due respect, but Jack and I are not enough. We all know that we'd never make it through the checkpoints with weapons of any sort and unless the plan is for us to use harsh language to get past Champer and his security detail."

Richards now continued. "We are well aware of the difficulties in smuggling things anywhere these days. Let's just say we have a plan that is well designed and we think likely to succeed."

Larry stared back at him for two beats. "A plan that requires two."

Richards smiled. "I'm not going to bullshit you, Larry. Ideally more than two, probably four or five. But we have learned over the years to work with what we have and based on how you availed yourself the other night and the fact that you did a pretty good job of getting the drop on us today, I think we can make it work with two."

Larry looked at Karen. "Another set-up?"

Karen stared back at him at first unsure of what he meant. She then worked it out. "Tonight? No, this was no set-up, Larry. You legitimately got the drop on us even if we did have Cory in the other room."

Nelson now spoke for the first time. "I needed a nap. The gunshot woke me up."

Larry nodded. "Okay, I'm in."

Kennex clapped his hands. "Fuckin' A!"

32

January 19th, 2033

Los Angeles, California

Kyle Jackson had learned to keep his head down over the years. He looked down at the various names of famous people on the sidewalk, most of them long dead, as he walked; although, he had memorized most of them.

He reached the corner of Hollywood and Vine and turned right. As usual, most people walked as he did, head down, avoiding making eye contact with one another and especially avoiding making eye contact with the soldiers who manned the turrets every few blocks.

He reflexively looked up and diagonally across the street at the large billboard that towered above the buildings. He had read it and others along the way almost every day for the past four years.

"Champer's Fourth Rule," it read and below it, "Report Anything Suspicious ,,, Anything."

Jackson looked back down and continued walking. He thought about Janie back at home. Her real name was Juanita and this was the very definition of something suspicious. Add to this Champer's first rule – all foreigners must register at the government office – and Jackson was a regular law breaker.

Kyle reached the grocery store. The Krogers sign still adorned the front; although, the company had collapsed along with many others when the world fell apart. Kyle knocked on the glass. He could see activity in the back of the store, but no came immediately to let him in.

Eventually, the manager, Joe Baker, a 60-something former army lieutenant, walked over and unlocked it for Kyle – the store was still a half-an-hour from opening.

"You're late, Jackson," said Baker as he opened the door.

Kyle looked down at Baker. Although Baker was probably six feet tall, Kyle was at least a half a foot taller than him – his large black frame and bald head cutting an imposing figure. Kyle then looked up at the digital clock that Baker had had installed the previous summer – it read 8:31.

"I've been knocking for a while."

"Bullshit, you're late. I'm going to dock you for the hour."

Kyle looked down again at Baker. He hated the man deeply. Baker had made it clear that he didn't like Mexicans as he called anyone of Latino descent or persons of color. He thought briefly about the pleasure he would take in crushing Baker's skull, but let it pass. He then nodded to Baker, who continued to block his route into the store.

"You know, Kyle – I was part of the invasion force back in 24. We killed a lot of your kind in the East LA uprising." Baker gave a satisfied smile.

Kyle continued to stare down at him. Kyle was a Navy Seal in a former life, but now he worked at a grocery store in the "New World". He had heard Baker brag about East LA a number of times over the past couple of years. He often liked to point this out to black and especially Latino customers, who complained about rations – "must have missed you in the East LA uprising, maybe next time."

Kyle smiled back. He had learned not to engage Baker as he knew he couldn't win and the risks were too great. He also knew that certain things got under Baker's skin and smiling back at him when he had said something self-satisfying was one of those things that got under Baker's skin.

Baker's smile turned to a brief frown. He moved out of Kyle's path and said, "you and Sanders get that fucking bathroom shined up, then man register four and you get to lock up tonight. Oh and Kyle?"

Kyle had started to walk past Baker and now turned back.

"Happy Martin Luther King day."

Kyle stared at Baker. He really could kill the man with his bare hands. For a moment, he felt the adrenalin surge. After two beats, the smile returned to his face. "Thanks, Mr. Baker."

An hour later, Kyle stood at register four. A middle-aged woman with a small girl sitting in her cart held out her ration card. Kyle took the card and scanned it. He looked at the screen on his register and waited for the computer to confirm all of the food he had scanned versus was what was allocated on her card. After ten-seconds of waiting, the computer declared in a metallic voice, "all clear."

Kyle nodded and smiled at the woman and winked at the little girl. The little girl smiled and the woman even seemed to allow herself a small upturn of the corners of her mouth.

An older black woman was next and Kyle scanned her goods one at a time.

The woman tapped the conveyor, getting Kyle's attention and she looked at a plastic bottle of pills that were next to her hand. Kyle recognized them as Prilosec, which were used to treat ulcers.

He made eye contact with the woman. She looked to be approaching 70 and she had seen better days. Her face was gaunt and her hands shook slightly. She mouthed to him, "please."

Kyle had been faced with these situations before. Technically, he could and should report the woman immediately. In fact, he could get in trouble simply for not reporting her attempted transgression. But Kyle was not in the business of reporting folks, his small if limited bit of protest against a world that he now mostly despised.

However, not reporting her and actually abetting her transgression were two different things. Kyle generally gave a polite almost imperceptible nod and the would-be criminal had in every prior instance, put the bottle of aspirin or extra box of cereal or head of lettuce in the "last-chance" basket that sat at the end of every register.

Kyle moved his head from side to side only slightly. The woman again mouthed "please", her eyes pleading with him. And then, "my husband", this time is a low whisper. Tears began to stream down her cheek.

Kyle took a deep breath. Although he did not look up, he knew the casino-like overhead cameras were always watching. Not only could Baker or one of his minions be watching, but the gestapo was known to do camera checks from time to time.

He looked down and scanned a tube of toothpaste. There were two more items to scan until the pills.

Kyle purposely knocked his pen to the ground. He needed a moment to gather his thoughts. He couldn't simply take the bottle and drop it in the bag as the exit scanners would pick it up as an un-scanned item. He felt for the pen and then closed his hand around it. He rose to a full standing position and scanned a bag of tomatoes.

The woman continued to stare at him, but Kyle no longer looked at her. He could feel her pleading eyes on him. He scanned two cans of baked beans and then grabbed the bottle of Prilosec.

Without hesitating, Kyle deftly moved the bottle over the scanner, keeping the RFID tag pointed away and in one motion brought it over the grocery bag. He used his powerful grip to crush the bottle, shooting the lid and the contents of the bottle into the bag. He moved his left hand to his side and reached with his right for a box of crackers. He held his breath for someone to call alarm to what he'd done, but nothing happened.

A minute later, he scanned the woman's ration card and a moment later the computer confirmed, "all clear." He had not made eye contact with her since he had moved the bottle, but he now looked at her. She said, "thanks, young man." She said it with little emotion; however, her eyes betrayed how deeply she appreciated what he'd done.

She pushed her cart out of the store; again, no alarms went off.

Kyle said, "Gary, I'm taking a quick break, back in five."

Gary Hellers replied, "no problem, big man."

Thirty seconds later, Kyle entered the men's room, the crushed bottle still in his pocket. His act of defiance may ultimately have consequences, as the monthly inventory would eventually reveal the missing bottle, but Kyle doubted they would figure it out. Despite the scanners, stuff disappeared every month and a bottle of ulcer pills was unlikely to lead to an investigation.

He hid the crushed bottle under a small space beneath one of the toilets. He had found the space a couple of months back when cleaning the floors and had thought at the time that it would make a good spot to stash something.

Kyle flushed the toilet and walked to the bathroom door. He smiled to himself – his little act of defiance felt good.

33

April 22nd, 2020

Youngstown, Ohio

Tony Salazar tried to tune out the yelling that came from behind him. The volume in his earpiece was turned up to maximum, but even then, he had trouble hearing Kim Stack's questions. Champer had done his usual best to fire up the crowd, but with the election fast approaching, the crowd appeared to be especially worked up tonight.

"I'm sorry, Kim, can you repeat the question?"

"Of course, Tony, I asked what the general mood of the crowd was tonight?"

Salazar nodded, an indication that he had heard the question, and then turned to look over his shoulder and pointed. "As you can see behind me, Kim, the crowd has been typically fired up to hear President Champer deliver the first speech of the campaign in which we know who his opponent will be, at least unofficially, this November. I would say the volume has been a bit higher than we have seen in some time."

Salazar's pointing at the crowd behind him further intensified the crowd's rage, and the chants of "CNN sucks" began. Throughout the evening, chants of "CNN sucks" had been intermixed with "Champ", "lock her up" and "witch hunt".

Salazar smiled as he waited for the next question. A couple of years earlier, the notion that a crowd of Americans would chant something like this at a US presidential rally would have been completely ludicrous to Salazar. Now, it was par for the course and he found it strange when he didn't hear the chants.

Someone from the edge of the ropes set up behind Salazar and other members of the media yelled, "stop smiling, Salazar, or we will wipe it off your face."

The man, who wore a red MAGA hat and a US army tee-shirt, said "Salazar" in a way meant to emphasize that it was Latino sounding.

Salazar heard the voice of his producer Brian Bennett, "Tony, we are going to go to a quick commercial and then come back to you."

Salazar nodded. The man behind him yelled again, "Salazar, I know you can hear me. You're the enemy." The man then began chanting, "Salazar sucks" and some in the crowd began to pick it up.

Salazar stared straight ahead. He had learned over the past few years not to engage people at

Champer's rallies as there was no upside in it for him to do so.

"Salazar, why don't you go back to Mexico!"

Salazar shook his head and turned to the man, who was about ten feet behind him. He stared at the man for about ten seconds and then said, "I'm from New Jersey, you fucking idiot."

Salazar instantly regretted saying it. He knew that the talking heads on Fox News, if they got a hold of it, would spin it in such a way that what Salazar had said was the worst thing ever said by a journalist in the history of the world and it was another indication that CNN hated regular Americans.

"We are back with Tony Salazar. Tony, what did we hear from Champer tonight?"

Salazar nodded. "Kim, we heard the usual attacks on the media as the enemy of the people, along with some of the highlights, at least as Champer sees them, of the past three-plus years. We also…"

"Tony!" Kim Stack yelled into Salazar's earpiece as the crowd behind Salazar surged over the ropes and engulfed him. She watched as at least ten people tackled Salazar under a flurry of kicks and punches.

Terry Kramer, Salazar's longtime cameraman, momentarily appeared in the frame as Stack stared at the screen in horror. "Tony!" she yelled again as Kramer attempted to pull people off of Salazar. The crowd soon turned on him and Kramer disappeared from the frame. A moment later, a hand or a hat was placed over the camera's lens and Stack could no longer see what was happening.

Salazar balled up in a fetal position as the kicks continued to pound away at his arms, legs, back and rib cage. One of his attackers was wearing steel-toed boots and Salazar could feel his ribs cracking as the boot was drawn back and thrust forward.

Salazar opened one eye and thought he saw Terry Kramer lying next to him. He had worked with Kramer for a decade and he and his wife were Godparents to Kramer's daughter, Nora.

Despite the pain of the blows raining in, Salazar began to crawl toward Kramer in an attempt to cover his friend. Salazar tried to crawl on his elbows, but this only seemed to intensify the crowd's rage and the pace of the blows began to pick up.

Salazar again balled up in an attempt to limit the damage. He could hear screaming all around him. He assumed that people were trying to pull the crowd off of him and Kramer, but if they were, it was not having much of an effect.

A moment later, the kicking stopped. Salazar could hear a voice trying to talk to him, but his ears were ringing and he could taste blood that was flowing from his mouth and nose.

Salazar turned his head to the side and saw Terry Kramer lying about three feet away. Kramer's eyes were open and staring vacantly. Blood was flowing freely from the top of his head. As Salazar fought to maintain consciousness, he wondered whether the steel-toed boots had been responsible for his friend's plight.

Off in what he thought was the distance, Salazar heard Kim Stack crying.

34

February 26th, 2011

New York, New York

"His birth certificate?"

Scott Burnside stared back at Richard Champer. The two of them sat in Champer's office on the top floor of Champer Tower in Manhattan. "That's what I said. A good chunk of the country, probably 25, maybe 30% believes that he was born in Africa, we want to fan that flame."

"You want me to run based on Obama not being an American?

Burnside took a swig from the bottle of Heineken that he held in his left hand. "I'm not even sure you should run yet, but I think this birther thing has some legs. People already doubt the government and birth certificates are probably the easiest thing to fake – at least that's what people believe. I mean, you are going back fifty years when there were no computers – who knows what's real and what's not."

Champer sipped from a glass of Dalmore single malt. "And you don't think people are going to accuse me of being a racist for this?"

Burnside smiled. "Of course they will. But those people aren't who we are after. We are looking to build a base of support – Champers if you will – and I think this birther thing is a good way to start the movement."

Champer now smiled. "So I go on Good Morning America and say what? Obama's an African?"

Burnside shrugged. "In a manner of speaking. You indicate to them that you are considering a run in 2012 and when they ask you about it, you subtly drop in that our President may not even be an American."

"The left will go ape-shit."

Burnside drained his beer. "That's the point," he paused, "for now."

35

November 3rd, 2021

Washington, District of Columbia

"Friends, in closing, I beg of you not to take this step. One of the few safeguards that remains for this great body, nay, this great institution and, perhaps, the last remaining check and balance on an Executive that has run amok for the past five-years is the ability of the minority to forestall legislation."

Senate Minority Leader, Scott Laird, paused and looked about the hallowed hall. He knew his words were powerless to stop the freight train that was rolling toward his party and the American people. Yet, he was going to get it on the record – history would record that he had tried his damnedest.

"We took away this right as it pertained to Federal judges. That blood is on my party's hands."

He paused again. "We took away that right as it pertained to Supreme Court judges. That blood is on the majority's hands."

He stared at the Majority Leader, Eric Douglas. The smug smile on his face told him that Douglas was relishing every moment of this speech. God will judge you, you ruthless prick, Laird thought to himself.

"The majority is now preparing to take away this right as it pertains to all matters of business that come before this esteemed body. I fear the road that we are rolling down will become a hill and that hill will become a mountainside and that mountainside will ultimately become a bottomless pit. A bottomless pit in which the will of the majority of this country's great citizens will be ignored."

He paused for his final flourish. "Here we stand ladies and gentlemen, friends. Here we stand on the one-year anniversary of the 2020 election, an election that saw all kinds of questionable things occur, none of which this body, nor any other has chosen to investigate. Here we stand with a President re-elected with nearly five million fewer votes than his opponent. Here we stand, and I am reminded of the final speech given more than 30-years ago by one of the greatest President's this country has ever had."

He looked about the chamber. "I am unfortunately reminded of this conservative lion's speech with a sense of sadness. For no longer are we a shining city on a hill; no longer a tall, proud city built on rocks stronger than oceans, wind-swept, God-blessed, and teeming with people of all kinds living in harmony and peace; no longer a city with free ports that hummed with commerce and creativity.

And no longer able to say that if that city had walls, the walls would have doors and the doors would be open to anyone with the will and the heart to get here."

He looked out at the crowd for a final time. "I beg you, in the name of Ronald Wilson Reagan - don't do this."

33-minutes later, Secretary of the Senate, Barry "Buck" Engles, struck the gavel three times. "The Vice-President casts the tie-breaking vote, by a vote of 51-50, the ayes have it."

And with that, the Senate filibuster was officially dead.

36

June 30th, 2034

Los Angeles, California

Karen stared at Larry. The other men had gone to sleep in the three of the four bedrooms off the main room. The two of them sat on the couch with a lamp in the corner providing the lone, dim light in the room. It was past midnight, but Karen felt wide awake.

They both held glasses of red wine, a rare indulgence in this day and age. Larry was not going to ask where it came from as he had not partaken in several years and he figured he'd just enjoy the guilty pleasure for a change. Larry took a sip of the wine. It wasn't particularly good, but he very quickly started to feel a warmth in his stomach that he could get used to. He decided to be uncharacteristically forward. "Tell me about you – I don't even know your last name."

Karen smiled and then said in her husky, yet feminine voice, "I'm fairly certain I don't know yours either, Larry."

She said "Larry" as though she was not sure that was his real name either. He decided to take the bait. "It is, in fact, Larry."

She smiled. "I thought so. You respond to it in such a way that suggests it's been your handle for a while."

"So it is Karen then?"

She took a sip of wine and then brushed her bangs off her forehead. Her blonde hair was cut short on the sides and back, but it was longer on top. Between her voice and her hair, Larry felt that she had embraced a blonde-haired version of "GI-Jane model" Demi Moore, which had been one of his favorites as a teenage boy in the 90s. "It was something else once."

"And the last name?"

She smiled. "For now, it's Keyes." She then paused and then seemed to decide she wanted to share more. "Let's just say that my real name carries some risks."

Larry took a sip of wine. "I can appreciate that."

She stared at him for several beats. "You've had some facial work done, Larry. Haven't you?"

Larry reflexively touched the area next to his right eye. He cursed himself silently for doing it. "What makes you say that?"

She squinted at him. "Because I'm good at this and because somehow your eyes don't quite match your face." She paused again and for second time in the past thirty-seconds, she shared more than she planned. "It's a kind face to be sure and one that I could very easily get used to, but not your face."

Larry was shocked that she had picked up on it. He had often stared in the mirror and thought the same thing, but he, of course, remembered what he used to look like. Here was a stranger that had picked up on it. "Okay, you know one of my secrets, tell me one of yours?"

Karen bit her lower lip and paused for a few beats. "I'll tell you what, I will tell you everything, but after."

Larry stared back at her. They had told him that the operation at the docks had been code named "Turning Point." He assumed that she planned to come clean after Turning Point. "Assuming somehow Jack and I survive this."

She smiled. "We have a good plan, one we have worked on since we found out that Champer was coming. After seeing you in action and knowing what Jack brings to the table, I think we have a good chance of success and the two of you getting out of there."

"When do I find out about this plan?"

"We will meet again in two nights – here – and we will fill in all of the gaps."

"And until then?"

She bit her lip again. "You stay here tonight, but go to work tomorrow and go back to your place tomorrow night."

Larry stared at her sensing a bit of regret in her voice at the idea they would be apart. He sipped the wine. "Are we sure my place is safe?"

She paused. "There's no reason to think otherwise. Our contacts in the gestapo do not suggest that what we did the other night elicited much traffic aside from some reports of gunshots fired. Your place should be clean."

Larry stared back at her. He had to admit he felt a twinge of regret at the thought of going back to his "normal life."

37

June 30th, 2034

Los Angeles, California

"Hey, Murph, have a look at this."

Detective Samuel Murphy sat at his desk reading the newspaper. While it was rare to see paper copies of newspapers anymore, especially in the OZ ("Occupied Zone"), Murphy knew and guy who knew a guy and he preferred the old school as opposed to reading his news on-line. He looked up at his sometime partner, Detective Mark Mason. "Whaddaya got?"

Mason smiled at Murphy's hackneyed phrase, which Mason had come accustomed to hearing from the man who was both his mentor in detective work and 24-years his senior. "Call up RAICS".

Murphy nodded and turned to his computer screen. "Lash, bring up RAICS."

The computer – Los Angeles System Helper or Lash – responded in a somewhat sexy female voice, "RAICS is now active."

Mason came around to stand next to Murphy so he could get a view of Murphy's screen. The screen declared Remote Artificial Intelligence Camera

System. Mason now spoke. "Lash, bring up file 227141."

Lash responded immediately, "227141 is now active."

The screen now showed an empty street. The crawl at the bottom indicated it was Sunset Boulevard, three days earlier and just after 5 AM. The feed ran for about 30-seconds and it shifted from one camera to the next, covering an area of about three blocks.

Murphy, who remained seated at his desk, looked up at Mason. "What am I looking at?"

Mason replied, "remember that shots fired report from the other day?"

Murphy squinted as if in thought, "not really."

Mason shook his head, "from the OIR that you are supposed to read every morning, but you instead choose to read that dinosaur on your desk." He pointed at the newspaper as he said this.

The OIR was the overnight incident report. Mason continued. "On Monday, the OIR mentioned three separate reports of shots fired in the area of Santa Monica and Reardon. It also mentioned reports of at least three men chasing another man."

Murphy stared at Mason, who had abruptly stopped speaking. "And what happened?"

Mason looked down at Murphy. "That's just it, nothing. A ram unit went in and did its usual rousting and didn't come up with anything."

Murphy stared at his one-time protégé. Mason was 32-years old and had been a detective for about four-years. Most of his world view was post-the war and he had only been a cop in the OZ. Murphy liked the man, but he also knew that Mason was a true believer and nothing he said or did was going to change that. "Okay, so why am I looking at the RAICS then?"

Mason frowned. "Well, the ram unit didn't find anything. I mean there were no bodies or anything and the hospitals didn't put in any reports of someone coming in with a GSW or anything, but ..." Mason purposely trailed off.

Murphy smiled. "Okay, I'll bite, but what?"

"The ram commander, Deke Ruckers, asked me to have a look and I found some interesting stuff, which made me dig a bit deeper."

Murphy squinted at the sound of Ruckers' name. He viewed him as nothing short of a Nazi, who relished the world we now lived in. "Go on."

Mason clapped his hands together. He was pleased with himself that he'd managed to tweak Murphy's interest. "Lash, bring up 212 Reardon."

The view on the screen shifted to the edifice of what looked to be a five or six story building.

"Okay, now what am I looking at?"

"Ruckers noted that this edifice got hit with something that was probably bullets."

"Did he find any spents?"

Mason shook his head. "No spent shells and no evidence that the markings on the buildings were actually bullet holes, but I went and had a look and if I had to say what it was under oath – I'd say someone shot the building four or five times."

Murphy stared at Mason waiting for him to continue. "That it?"

Mason smiled again pleased that Murphy was interested even though his interest was waning. "Well, no. As I said, the markings convinced me that the reports were probably accurate, so I checked out 212. And guess what I found?"

Murphy thought at first it was a rhetorical question, but after several seconds he realized it was not. He said with way too much excitement, "what?"

Mason smiled. "In the foyer of the building, I found what looks to be another bullet hole from the same gun that was fired at the outside of the building."

"Shells?"

Mason shook his head. "No, but if these were professionals, they were obviously pretty thorough with that. I would also have to say that whatever happened in the foyer of that building, someone cleaned it up pretty good because when I painted it with the iScanner, it looked like you could have eaten off the floor."

"Is that it?"

Mason looked back at the computer. "Lash, bring up 227136."

"227136 is now active."

They were now looking again at 212 Reardon. The time stamp indicated it was 5:08 AM.

"Lash, run on continuous loop."

The two men stared at the screen. After about 30-seconds, Murphy spoke. "Mark, what the fuck am I looking at?"

Mason looked down at Murphy. "You don't see it?"

"See what?"

Mason pointed at the screen. "That guy!"

Murphy looked at the screen. Someone was clearly looking out the window; although only the top of his or her head was visible. The head disappeared and then reappeared a moment later.

"Lash, go to 227137 and run on continuous loop."

"227137 is now active."

It was 212 Reardon, but at 5:10 AM. Murphy continued to stare at the window that Mason had identified. "Wait, what was that?"

Mason pumped his fist. "Yes! That my friend is the door opening and closing. You are seeing the light from the hallway briefly spill into the room."

"Lash, go to 227138 and run on continuous loop."

"227138 is now active."

It showed 212 Reardon at 5:12 AM. Again, the distinctive light from the hall spilled into the room for a moment and then disappeared.

Murphy looked up at Mason. "Okay, take me through it."

Mason pulled over a chair from an empty desk and sat down. He rubbed his hands together and smiled. "Okay, so someone is being chased. We don't have it on any of the cameras, but as you well know there is a ten-second cycle every minute in which the AI evaluates what it sees and then resets, storing the footage if there is nothing to see in the cloud. We know that there are groups out there that have figured out how to time the RAICS, so not getting them on film is not all that surprising."

Murphy nodded. "Okay."

Mason continued. "So someone is being chased and shot at and they end up at 212 Reardon and they end up in this guy's apartment and soon after they leave."

Murphy stared at Mason for several beats. "I am assuming you went to this guy's apartment."

Mason smiled and almost looked like he was jumping up and down in the chair. "Correct and guess what I found?"

"Oh for fuck's sake, please tell me."

Mason gave a brief pouty look. "Nothing. I went to the apartment and while it's lived in – pajamas on the floor, bed has been slept in; whoever lives there lives a pretty lean life. Not all that unusual these days, but pretty sparse even for the OZ."

"And?"

Mason smiled. "So I turned over the fuckin' place and in the bottom of the closet against the back wall was a hidden space. Probably would have missed it, but something seemed slightly off about the paint, so I pounded it with the butt of my Smith and found it."

"Found what?"

"A box with shells for a Glock, including four clips, night vision goggles, a scope for what I'm guessing would be a sniper rifle; although, there was no rifle, some other tac gear and several IDs for a guy that alternatively goes by the names Dan LaRussa, John Lawrence and Carl Weathers."

Murphy started laughing.

"What?"

Your mystery man has a thing for karate and boxing movies.

"Huh?"

Murphy shook his head. "Forget it. Who rents the place?"

"The Lawrence guy."

"I'm assuming we have staked the place and he hasn't been back?"

Mason shook his head. "And the OZID records on John Lawrence are a complete dead end. It has a record of him renting at 212 Reardon, but everything else seems to be total bullshit. He's supposed to work at a hardware store, but the owners have never heard of him, he dutifully reports to various checkpoints, but none of the soldiers recognize his photo, etcetera, etcetera."

Murphy frowned. It was not easy to trick the Occupied Zone Information Database, so whoever John Lawrence was, he wasn't messing around.

Murphy stared at Mason for several beats. "Okay, so let me see if I understand this. Someone is being chased and shot at. We don't get it on video, but we are pretty sure it happened. This all ends at 212 Reardon where whoever is chased, ends up. This Lawrence guy or whatever the hell his name is, lets the person in and soon after leaves with them. That it?"

Mason nodded. "So far."

Murphy put his head in his hands and rubbed for a few seconds. "Okay, I think it's worth looking into. I think we need to determine whether this person that was running meant to hook up with Lawrence, which seems pretty obvious given that they'd have to be pretty fuckin' lucky to stumble on what looks to be a pretty capable guy, but we should try to make certain. At the same time, we need to talk to Jerry about how one could fool the OZID and see if he has any ideas about locating this guy."

Mason clapped his hands together again. "I am so proud of myself."

Murphy laughed. "Baby steps, Daniel-son, baby steps."

38

August 29th, 2023

Warsaw, Poland

Constantin Kassov's palms were sweating. It was stifling in the T-16 Armata, the latest in Russian tank technology, and Kassov tried to focus on the computer screen in front of him.

The terrain flew by on the screen. This was not your grandfather's tank, but rather a fleet fighting machine that could travel at speeds up to 100 kilometers an hour. They had crossed out of Belarus nearly two hours before and Kassov was now focused on the screen, awaiting the outlines of Warsaw. His number two, Pavel Garpev, who was focused on his own screen spoke. "Still in formation."

Kassov nodded. The vague outlines of Warsaw then began to materialize on his screen. "Prepare to engage."

Sergei Petroff, Kassov's longtime gunner, acknowledged the order. He keyed in the coordinates for the unmanned turret, which fired 125 mm smoothbore cannon.

Kassov heard the four distinct clicks in his headset. "Engage."

Almost simultaneously, 35 T-16's fired. Up above, laser guided smart bombs began to rain down on the city. Within minutes, the death toll would climb into the tens of thousands.

Mother Russia was reclaiming her lost children.

39

September 3rd, 2023

Lexington, Kentucky

The crowd was restless. Five other states - New Jersey, Connecticut, Maryland, Washington and Oregon - had joined New York in supporting California. The Russian invasion of Eastern Europe had gone unanswered by NATO and Champer's flagship property in Manhattan had been badly damaged by vandals. Culminating what had been a disastrous two months for Champer, the "pansy-ass PM" from Canada had seemed to indicate in an interview of his own that Canada would "welcome any outlaws" with open arms.

Through it all, Champer had kept silent. His Twitter account was still active, of course, but Burnside had advised him to lay low. Elections were won in the last two months after all and there was no point in making a big flourish in the middle of August when no one was watching.

It had taken all of Champer's intestinal fortitude not to lash out in public, but he had made it to Labor Day. Burnside had sketched out what the next two months would look like and Champer was excited about getting back in front of his adoring crowds.

Champer prepared to come out on stage. Vice-President Partridge was out there trying to fire up the crowd, but they were already in a frenzy, looking for blood, so even the normally staid Partridge seemed to have them going. "Friends, I would like to introduce the man who has indeed made this country great again and continues to keep it great every day. The 45th President of these United States – Richard Harrison Champer!" Partridge made a point of emphasizing "united" as he said the last part.

The crowd roared and Champer strode out on stage, head upright and made a bee-line to Partridge. He shook the man's hand and made a point of pulling him close. "Thanks, Petey," he said loudly into Partridge's ear. Champer then strode to the podium.

The crowd chanted "Champ" and then "Beachum Sucks". Champer drank it all in as he pointed at various people in the crowd mouthing the word, "thank you" as he nodded. He didn't thank anyone in particular, but rather had learned that it made him look more human to look at least a little bit humble in front of such adoration.

After several minutes of chants and cheers, he raised his hands to quiet the crowd. There was no teleprompter. He would do what he did best – go off the cuff.

"So the media folks, they've been all up in arms about Russia. It's Russia this and Russia that. You know what, folks? Europe has been at war for two thousand years and it's going to be at war for two thousand more years. The media and you know what I call them, don't you folks?"

The crowd chanted on command, "fake news, fake news, fake news."

Champer smiled. "That's right, folks, they're the fake news. Everything that they say is a lie and they are trying to make it seem like Russia was not provoked and we know that's a lie, don't we, folks?"

The crowd continued to roar with approval.

"And you know what's the most amazing thing, folks? You don't know? Of course, you know. The fake news cares more about what's happening in some far off place where you can't pronounce anyone's name and they probably hate our country than they do about what is happening in this country."

"They hate our country just like the media hates this country."

The crowd booed as Champer emphasized the media and hate.

He now turned to California and Governor Beachum. "Beachum! What kind of name is Beachum? Like something a whale would do. Anyway, speaking of hating our country, you know what he did? We know what he did, don't we folks?"

The crowd once again began chanting "Beachum sucks."

"That son-of-a-bitch, oh wait, I'm not supposed to say that." He mock covered his mouth and then continued. "Screw them, am I right? Screw them. That son-of-a-bitch decides to take his elitist cabal and that's what it is folks – it's a cabal. I like that word "cabal". He said it very slowly, making sure the movement of his mouth was exaggerated. "You don't hear it very much, I think. But that's what Beachum and his elitist cronies are – they are a cabal and they are trying to overthrow this country."

The crowd began booing loudly and then someone yelled out "kill" and within seconds, the crowd had taken up a "kill" chant.

Champer smiled and put his hands up again. "No, we don't want to hurt anyone." He paused. "Unless we have to," he added with a comic flourish. The crowd once again started chanting "kill".

"Folks and now it's not just Beachum and his cabal, but we've got that bitch from New York saying the same thing," the crowd roared at his use of "bitch" and then took up the "bitch" chant.

"I'm not supposed to say that either. It's not presidential, but you know what? We are remaking what it means to be presidential, aren't we folks?"

Champer continued for some time, attacking California, New York, the other states and even mentioning Canada. The crowd continued to be whipped up in a frenzy. He then turned to the vote.

"So they think they are going to hold a vote. Maybe they hold a vote, maybe we let them do that." He paused. "Maybe we don't, I don't know."

He then paused for several beats and the crowd quieted. They could sense that something big was coming.

Champer now toned it down several notches. "Maybe we let them hold the vote. My Cabinet is telling me not to let them hold the vote, but maybe I will – I don't know." He paused. "But I got news for you, folks."

The anticipation in the room was now palpable. They had seen this script before. "I got news for you. If they hold this vote. No, screw it, when they hold this vote." His voice was now rising. "When they hold this vote and if they decide to declare war on the United States, maybe we go ahead and use the full might and force of the US military to make them bow the knee before us!"

The crowd roared and Champer pumped his fist. "Bow the knee!" He screamed and now the crowd took up the chant, "bow the knee, bow the knee, bow the knee."

At the side of the stage, Vice-President Partridge continued to smile. His eyes said something different.

40

October 26th, 2022

Springfield, New Jersey

Scott Laird sat silently watching the television screen. He wasn't sure if he had failed, but he sure felt like a failure. He had spent what he thought was his last ounce of energy on winning back control of the Senate in the 2020 election, but somehow, despite math that appeared to be in the Democrats favor and a deeply unpopular President, the best he could manage was a 50/50 split.

With Champer getting re-elected, Partridge was once again the decisive vote, which had caused the dominoes to start to fall.

First, the Supreme Court had continued to shift to the right with six seats now firmly in the hands of Conservative justices. Then, the filibuster has once and for all been put to death. And finally Congress had decided to promulgate 101-64, a Federal law that effectively linked Federal funding for education to abortion restrictions.

He had to admit that 101-64 was an artful solution. Rather than come out and say abortion is illegal, which would have run firmly into the buzz saw of states' rights issues, Congress had basically made it a choice – receive billions in federal funding for education or adopt what had become known as "the Douglas Standard" after Senate Majority Leader Eric Douglas.

While the Douglas Standard still allowed for abortions to occur, it was so restrictive so as to make it likely that any state that wanted to provide for safe access to abortions would be in violation of the Standard.

In a normal world, Laird would have been confidant that the Supreme Court would have stuck down the statute on the grounds that there was no relationship between federal funding for education and a woman's right to choose.

Once upon a time, the federal government had tried to tie highway funding to a drinking age of 21 and while the Court had upheld the linkage in *South Dakota v. Dole*, it had laid out some fairly tight restrictions for such linkages in its majority opinion.

Laird had held out hope that the "Dole Standard" would prevail. His hope was fleeting.

Laird removed his glasses and continued to stare at the screen. Across the bottom, the CNN banner declared "Supreme Court Declines to Hear New Jersey vs. United States, 101-64 Now Law of the Land".

By refusing to hear the case, the Supreme Court had effectively removed a woman's right to choose in most of the country.

Laird sat back. He had no doubt that states such as California and his home state of New York would try to make it work, but Federal funding for education ran into the tens of billions. It would be very hard to sell starving the schools of funds in favor of continuing to provide safe access to abortions. He cursed just how much better the other side was at politics than was his side.

41

October 27th, 2022

Gary, Indiana

Vice-President Peter Partridge stared out his kitchen window. He liked to come home as often as possible as he had come to hate Washington in his six-years as VP. While it seemed quaint, he loved doing the regular things such as washing the dishes and fixing stuff around the house, which was not an option when in DC. He often harped to his wife Allison that it was one of the few releases he had left.

"What are you daydreaming about?" Allison Partridge had walked into the kitchen; although, as Partridge often noted about his wife, she did not as much walk into a room as sweep into a room.

Partridge snapped out of his brief dalliance with his thoughts and looked over his shoulder. He continued to rinse a plate in the warm soapy water.

"Was just thinking that lawn needs to be mowed."

Allison Partridge gave a smug smile. "I'm sure you were."

She walked over and wrapped her arms around him. Partridge put down the plate and hung his head.

"What's wrong, Pete?"

Partridge shook his head. "Nothing's wrong."

Allison reached up and turned her husband's chin. "Bull crap, Mr. Vice-President."

Partridge smiled. "You kiss my kids with that potty mouth?"

Allison squinted and stared at him. "Every day, sometimes more than once."

After sharing a kiss, the two of them moved to the kitchen table as Allison poured two cups of black coffee.

After about 30-seconds of silence, Allison spoke. "Seriously, Pete, what is it?"

Partridge stared back at his wife of 23-years. After about ten seconds of silence, he decided to give her a partial answer. "Not sure."

Allison put down her coffee and reached across to grasp Pete's hand. "You've gotten everything we wanted, haven't you?"

Partridge stared back. When he had accepted the VP nomination more than six-years earlier, he had never expected Champer to win. Rather, he had done so because he and Allison had figured it would be a good springboard for a run at the White House in 2020 if the chips fell the right way.

When Champer had somehow pulled it out, Partridge had thought briefly about resigning at some point during his first term. He hated everything about Champer and could barely stand to be in the same room as the President, let alone keep a permanent smile plastered to his face every time Champer spoke publicly and insisted Partridge stand behind him.

He and Allison had debated the merits of resigning and had decided that it would probably ruin his chances at ever running nationally again and potentially would end his political career in Indiana. They also saw another angle.

Partridge looked at Allison. "Have we?"

Allison smiled. "You came to Washington to change things for the better. While Champer and Douglas will get the credit, it was you that finally did away with abortion. The history books may not remember this, but if there is a higher power, he will."

Partridge nodded and gave a half-hearted smile. "Maybe. But I'm also worried about what else he might remember."

Allison sipped her coffee. "You've got nothing to be ashamed of, Pete."

Partridge stared back at her. "You don't really believe that, Ali, do you? I mean, how much have I turned my back on these past six-years? How many times have I stood and smiled for the cameras when the President said something despicable? How many times have I ignored what was right in front of my nose?"

Allison shook her head. "You made sacrifices for the causes you believed in. And in two-years, you will be President and you will be able to right some of the wrongs."

Partridge took a deep gulp of the coffee. He could feel it burn his tongue slightly. He looked again out the window above the sink. From his vantage point at the table, he could no longer see the lawn, but just a few wisps from the red cedar that towered in front of the house.

Partridge then looked back at his wife. "How many more wrongs am I going to have to look past until we get there?"

Allison Partridge simply stared back at her husband.

42

April 30th, 2011

Washington, District of Columbia

"Richard Champer is here tonight. Now I know that he's taken some flak lately. But no one is happier— no one is prouder—to put this birth certificate matter to rest than The Champ. And that's because he can finally get back to focusing on the issues that matter: Like, did we fake the moon landing? What really happened in Roswell? And where are Biggie and Tupac?"

The White House Correspondent's Dinner crowd roared with laughter and President Obama continued. "All kidding aside, obviously we all know about your credentials and breadth of experience. For example ... no seriously, just recently, in an episode of Celebrity Apprentice, at the steakhouse, the men's cooking team did not impress the judges from Omaha Steaks. And there was a lot of blame to go around, but you, Mr. Champer, recognized that the real problem was a lack of leadership, and so ultimately you didn't blame Lil Jon or Meat Loaf, you fired Gary Busey. And these are the kinds of decisions that would keep me up at night. Well handled, sir. Well handled. Say what you will about Mr. Champer, he certainly would bring some change to the White House. Let's see what we've got up there."

The crowd applauded with many craning their necks this way and that to get a look at Champer.

Champer sat stoically, a slight smirk on his face. I will get this motherfucker, he thought to himself. So, help me, God, I will get this motherfucker.

43

July 1st, 2034

Long Beach, California

Larry tried to treat the work day just like any other day. At lunch, he had a run-in with Greg Pierson, who was one of those guys that liked to randomly give someone a hard time every now and again and today it happened to be Larry's turn.

Pierson was a former marine who had been "mistreated" by an IED back in Afghanistan. He walked with a limp as a result and nearly 25-years later, he had become a bitter man, who blamed his injuries and the state of the world on pretty much everyone else.

Pierson also happened to live a couple of blocks from Larry, so they would see each other from time to time outside of work; although, Larry made a point of not doing much more than nodding at Pierson when he saw him. The two of them also had a remarkably similar look, at least until one got a really close look.

Larry used to wonder why a guy like Pierson had not simply left California after the takeover. He was ex-military and undoubtedly had voted for Champer and against secession, so it would not have been hard to get out. Who would voluntarily want to live in a police state?

Eventually, Larry had figured that the government encouraged people like Pierson to stay, as it helped to have those sympathetic to the cause mixed in with the masses, who were not.

Larry almost never engaged his coworkers in any banter and Pierson had decided today to make a point of that. He had questioned Larry on what his problem was with the rest of them and Larry had simply smiled back and assured Pierson that there was no problem.

Pierson had then pointed out that Larry was even more of a prick away from work and Larry again had just smiled back.

Thankfully, Pierson had left it at that as the last thing Larry needed was to get involved in an incident of some sort. Larry finished the work day quietly; although, he could feel Pierson's eyes on him from time to time.

Larry almost never ran into much of a line-up at the four checkpoints he had to pass through on the way to work in the morning. He usually hit the first checkpoint at just before 7 AM and with the curfew keeping most people off the streets before 6 AM and the general early hour, there was almost never much of a build-up.

The way home was a different story as Larry got off work at 5 PM (although it had been moved up to 4:30 to allow people to get home before curfew). With all non-essential car traffic off limits in the Occupied Zone, one had to walk or take public transportation to work, which had most people converging at the checkpoints (choke-points as they were jokingly referred to) at around the same time.

Larry's first checkpoint going home was actually at the entrance to the Long Beach docks and most of the guys on the 8-to-5 shift had figured out how to stagger their arrivals, so the line never got too bad.

Checkpoint two was a different story as it not only picked up lots of dockworkers, but it also picked up a fair bit of traffic from industrial town and from the various consumer shops along the way.

Just beyond the checkpoint was the bus depot that would take the masses back to Los Angeles.

Larry kept his head down and shuffled forward. The line normally took about 15-minutes, but today it was a little bit slower. As he reached the checkpoint, he noted two uniformed gestapo cops amongst the regular soldiers. Larry stifled a small smile as the cops instantly made him think of fat man and little boy as one was grossly overweight and the other was barely five-feet tall.

Larry dutifully handed his papers to the checkpoint guard, a 20-something brown-haired kid with a crewcut and an honest looking face. The kid was sweating under the 90 degree heat in his army fatigues and unlike some of his comrades, he seemed to generally have a good demeanor and was not just trying to roust people.

The kid looked over Larry's papers and then he said, "look up and left, please."

Larry was surprised by the request, but he dutifully obeyed, making eye contact with the gestapo cops as he looked left. They held an iPad and looked at its screen and then back at Larry.

"He's clear," said "fat man",

The guard handed Larry back his papers, "thank you, sir."

Larry nodded to the guard as he took back his papers. He'd be roughly the Spooner's age he thought to himself.

As he passed, he was unable to catch sight of the image of John Lawrence on the iPad screen.

44

October 3rd, 2020

San Jose, California

Dimitri opened the door to the air conditioned sub-chamber within Ameridyne Systems. He loved the poetry of the name – call it hiding in plain sight.

During the day, Ameridyne's 450 employees developed web-hosting solutions for small and medium sized businesses. While not a huge player in the $50 billion industry, Ameridyne was nicely profitable, which helped to fund a number of clandestine endeavors.

At night, a smaller subset of Ameridyne's employees worked on a different project, which had been simply code named "Identity." Four shifts of ten hours rotated each night with eight men on each team and forty working on the project all together, so that each team worked every fourth day with one rotation off every fourth week.

Not all were Russians. In fact, nearly half were Eastern European and another seven were actually Americans. Thoroughly vetted and handsomely paid, Dimitri did not doubt their loyalty to the project.

Dimitri, of course, worried about leaks. While the men were loyal, they were still human and what they were working on had enormous "holy shit" implications as Dimitri liked to say.

However, in many ways the American Administration and its allies in Congress had made it very easy on Dimitri and his Russian bosses.

In the 2016 Election, the Russians had quite overtly tried to influence the Election, including meetings with members of Champer's team and, of course, Champer's own son. The approach in 2016 had been quite crude as Dimitri reflected on it – they had spent less than $20 million to help elect a President of the United States malleable to Russian influence. They didn't even try very hard to hide their tracks.

Instead of launching a thorough investigation to get to the bottom of what happened in the 2016 Election and, of course, to make sure that it didn't happen again, the Administration and many in Congress had bent over backwards to deny anything had happened and to obfuscate any investigation that might take place.

In the end, the "Cullen probe", which had been named after Special Prosecutor Paul Cullen, had been an inconvenience that ended up leading to some indictments. But the Americans had largely missed what was hiding just under their noses, which was a testament to the stubbornness of the American political system.

Dimitri had now been in America for more than 25-years. He loved the freedoms it provided, but he was forever loyal to Mother Russia.

He had been surprised by 2008 and the election of Barrack Obama. He would never have thought the Americans would nominate, let alone elect an African American President, but the combination of the Global Financial Crisis and the oration skills of Obama had created the perfect storm.

He smiled when he thought about what they had pulled off in 2016 and the way the American political system had treated the subsequent investigation. As he had liked to say to his colleagues – could you imagine if Obama had done half the things Champer had done – what would the Republican Congress's reaction have been?

Rather than bury its head in the sand, as Congress had chosen to do with most of what Champer had done and been accused of doing, it would have been a merry-go-round of investigations.

History was written by the victors – indeed.

Dimitri walked around the room and then made eye contact with Ilya Karpov, who was the head of the Identity project and the man who had summoned Dimitri to Ameridyne.

Karpov pointed at a small conference room and after doing one more walk around of the room in which Charlie Team worked on the project, Dimitri crossed to meet Karpov.

He shut the door and warmly embraced Karpov, who kissed Restanov on both cheeks. "Dimitri, please sit."

Restanov sat across from Karpov, who had a big smile on his face. "Dimitri, I think we've got it."

Dimitri let out a breath. While he was not a man to stress about many things, with Election Day roughly four-weeks away, he had begun to worry. The efforts they had used in 2016 and 2018 had been stepped up once again, but social media had gotten smarter and there was a lot less dirt on Pat Dyson, the Democratic candidate, than there was the last time around.

Further, Champer was deeply unpopular. The economic slowdown that began in late 2019 helping to bring down his already substandard approval rating. Even with the best efforts of Mother Russia, there was a good chance he'd lose.

Dimitri smiled. "I knew you would – tell me." He then paused. "In English."

Karpov smiled back. He knew Dimitri was no expert on technology and so he got the gist immediately of what he meant by "in English".

"Okay, so it was Beta Team that had the breakthrough. They came up with the basic algorithm that will allow us to infiltrate all, some or none of the machines."

Dimitri nodded. "So we can target as we see fit?"

Karpov nodded back. "Exactly. And the simplicity of it is nothing short of artwork."

Dimitri smiled. "Tell me."

Karpov paused. He was clearly searching for a way to explain the process in a way that Restanov would follow. "Okay, as you know our biggest problem has been that voting machines are not connected to the Internet. Essentially every machine needs to have the voting software uploaded to it by hand via the insertion of a hard disk."

Dimitri nodded. "I am still with you."

Karpov smiled. "Okay and the alternative, which is attacking the voting rolls, which is easy, is really not that appealing because all we end up doing is changing the identity information of registered voters, but that doesn't stop the precincts from allowing these people to vote and then confirming the information later."

"So, what you are saying is – we could target precincts in close races likely to vote Democrat, but there is no guarantee that those who should be disqualified from voting because we changed their information are actually barred from voting."

Karpov nodded. "Exactly, which brings us back to hacking the machines."

Dimitri made a face. "But you just said we can't do that."

Karpov smiled. "No, I said they were not connected to the Internet, making a traditional hack impossible. However, what is not impossible and is, in fact, quite simple, is to give a bunch of people a free Starbucks card."

"A Starbucks card?"

Karpov nodded. "A Starbucks card. So, what we did was to focus on the phishing side of the hack and we came up with a targeted Trojan horse of sorts that gives everyone who clicks on it a $10 Starbucks card."

Dimitri made the face again. "So we are going to give 125 million Americans a Starbucks card?"

Karpov smiled. "No, comrade. We are going to give about 3,000 people a Starbucks card. In fact, we already have."

"Go on."

"As you know, one of the focuses of our 2016 and 2018 operations was to make sure we hacked as many of the operations of the state voting commissions as we could. We didn't need to get in, but we needed to make sure we had access to real-time updates on who worked there."

Dimitri nodded. "I recall."

"So, we hit all of these people – about 3,000 – with our Starbucks promotion, which is a completely legitimate promotion."

"But?"

Karpov slapped the table between them. "But, when they click on the promotion, which looks like it comes from Starbucks, they also implant a Trojan horse in their state's voting system. The virus instantly infects their network, but is so artfully written that it is nearly undetectable by even the most sophisticated systems and as we well know – most state voting commissions are the antithesis of sophistication."

"But, the voting machines are still not connected to this?"

"No they're not, but the voting software that will be uploaded to the voting machines is – so when they insert their discs into the machines, we have infiltrated their system."

Dimitri smiled.

Karpov held up a finger. "Wait, it gets better. While we can essentially infect almost every voting machine, we run the risk of being too obvious. In other words, Champer needs to win, but we don't want to make it blatantly obvious that the results make absolutely no sense at all."

Karpov paused to have a drink of water and then continued. "So, we came up with a simple workaround. Rather than target every machine, we only target those precincts that were reasonably close the last time, but went against Champer. We constructed a program that only targets precincts that went between 40% and 50% for Champer in 2016 and we give him 55% of the vote this time in those precincts. Since we are only altering the close precincts, we shouldn't bring about any really strange outcomes."

Dimitri interjected. "The Buchanan problem."

Karpov nodded. "Exactly."

When Pat Buchanan came close to winning some Florida precincts back in the 2000 presidential election, it became clear very quickly that something was wrong with the ballots that somehow increased his vote totals. It turned out because Florida used a butterfly ballot, Al Gore's name was directly across from Pat Buchanan's with the voting circles between their names. Someone wishing to vote for Gore would fill in a circle directly above that of Buchanan and considering the advanced age of many in Florida, it was easy to make a mistake in one's vote. Almost all of these "mistakes" would have gone against Gore and he lost the state and ultimately the Election by less than 1,000 Florida votes.

Dimitri studied Karpov for a moment. "How do we know if this will be enough?"

Karpov put his arms out in an "I don't know gesture". "We cannot say for sure it will be enough. But if we take the states that Champer won narrowly in 2016 and the states he lost narrowly and run the math, he wins in nearly every computer simulation that we have run."

"And without it?"

"Our simulations suggest that he stands virtually no chance of reelection."

Dimitri frowned. "So, if he is to lose in a landslide, which is possible, then there is nothing we can do to stop this. But if the election is meant to be even remotely close, then we are likely to prevail?"

Karpov nodded. "Exactly, my friend, exactly."

Dimitri sat back in his chair and stared out the window of the small boardroom at the men working. He didn't love unknowns and his bosses liked them even less. But Champer was his own worst enemy in a number of ways, beginning with, but certainly not ending with his Twitter account.

"See if you can figure out a way to increase the odds, Ilya."

Karpov stared at him for several seconds and then simply nodded.

45

July 1st, 2034

Los Angeles, California

"And Mark figured this out by himself?"

Murphy smiled at his wife. He could tell from the tone of her voice that she highly doubted Mason could crack an egg, let alone the John Lawrence file. The two of them sat on the couch in the living room of their modest house in what used to be known as Sherman Oaks. "As far as I know. Guess he had a good teacher."

Emma Murphy smiled at her husband. "That's a given, but from what you just described, that was some genuine detective work he pulled off. What did Jerry Lane say?" Jerry Lane ran the IT group.

"He said it would have taken some very sophisticated tech to fool OZID. Not impossible mind you, but for John Lawrence to exist, but not really exist at the same time would take someone who is well funded and has a real secret to hide."

Emma took a sip from a glass of white wine. While alcohol was hard to get, being a cop's wife had its privileges even if she was not a big fan anymore of what Sam did. She snuggled a bit into the couch. "So what's next?"

Sam took a deep gulp from his can of Budweiser. "We have put John Lawrence's picture at all the checkpoints and we have his place staked out. Aside from that, there's not much we can do as despite the thousands of cameras we have in this friggin city, we can't seem to get a hit on this guy."

Emma now stared at her husband for a few beats. "Are we sure we want to catch this guy?"

Sam sighed and stared back at his wife. Even though he was sure he knew what she meant, he asked the question. "What do you mean, Em?"

She gave him her unhappy face. "I think you know what I mean, Samuel. You are 58-years old and you are two years from mandatory retirement. You also hate pretty much everything about the world we now live in and when we still held elections in California, you generally voted for the other guy."

Sam sighed again. "So what, I don't help Mark to catch this guy?"

"Catch him for what? From what you described, it's not even clear that he actually did anything!"

"Aside from three fake IDs, a bunch of bullets, some tac gear and tricking an un-trickable computer system."

She smiled. "Yes, aside from that." She paused. "Seriously, Murph. Something feels like you back off on this one. I'm not sure it's because I think I want to root for this guy whatever he's up to ..." she paused again and took Sam's hand. "...Or because I'm worried that if you go up against him, you'll lose."

Murphy took another gulp of his beer. He stared into the empty bottle for several beats. "I'm not so sure either."

46

July 1st, 2034

Los Angeles, California

Larry came up Reardon from the other side of Sunset. It was still roughly 25-minutes until curfew, so he had some time before he had to seek shelter.

As he approached the corner of Sunset and Reardon, he could see no obvious signs of surveillance on his place. An army Humvee shot by him, turning hard on Sunset. Larry made a point of not looking at it – you learned your lessons over the years.

Aside from the Humvee, which was now fading in the distance, there was no other traffic on the road. Larry knew the cameras were always watching and standing on the corner made him a bit of a sore thumb, so he continued his slow shuffle on the side opposite to 212 Reardon.

The Reardon Butcher was almost directly across the street from his place. Larry had some meat rations left on his ration card, so he had decided that he would stop there to get a final look at his place before making a decision.

He shuffled up the street and turned into the butcher shop.

One of the benefits from his vantage point of the Occupied Zone was the lack of auto traffic. There were still cars parked on the roads to be sure, but compared to how it had been before the war, traffic was generally thin. Add to this the curfew in the wake of the Santa Monica massacre and it was not hard to see whether the gestapo had set up any sort of trap.

The cameras were another story. Larry realized they could watch his place without actually having a presence on the street. But he also knew how to fool the cameras.

After ordering some sliced turkey and pepperettes, Larry handed over his ration card and $14. He had decided he was going to go for it.

Larry left the butcher shop and crossed slowly to his building. He opened the door leading in and paused for a moment in the foyer. It didn't take an investigative expert to discern that someone had checked the area. It could have been FOB or the gestapo or both. As Larry walked toward the stairs (had it really been less than a week since he was sliding through the lobby?), he looked up and caught site of where the bullet from the doorman had hit the ceiling.

Larry trudged up to the second floor. He stopped at apartment 21 and knocked. Jessica Rosen answered the door within seconds.

"Hey, John," she said while biting her lower lip. "I'm surprised to see you."

Larry raised his eyebrows, but decided to wait to ask. "How's Annie?" Annie was Jessica's seven-year old daughter.

"She's okay. She's with Silvio this week."

Silvio was Jessica's ex-husband. Larry had made a point of keeping to himself these past five years. But one night, about three years earlier, Silvio, who was an ex-marine that had lost a chunk of his thigh in the war, had gotten too deep into his bourbon rations, when they were still rationing alcohol.

Over the two or so years he had lived at 212, Larry had crossed paths with Jessica and seen the telltale signs of abuse. His heart bled for her, but he had his own problems and responsibilities, so he had kept his head down.

That night, Larry could tell that the yelling in apartment 21 was morphing into something worse. He decided to go and casually knock on the door, but no one answered. Through the door, he could hear Annie crying and the distinctive sound of someone whose mouth was being muffled. Larry didn't wait for his better judgement, but kicked open the door instead.

Silvio was standing behind Jessica holding her neck with one hand and her mouth with the other. Larry had calmly told him to let her go and Silvio had reluctantly agreed. He then ran at Larry, who casually flipped Silvio to the floor, despite his much larger size, and kept his knee pressed against the back of his head.

He then instructed Silvio on how it was going to go from here and that Jessica and Annie were now under his protection. Larry finished his instruction calmly and coldly with, "you do understand that if a hair is out of place on these two wonderful ladies that I will find you and kill you?" He then pressed his Glock, which he had not revealed until then, against the side of Silvio's head.

Despite his head being pressed against the floor, Silvio managed to nod. Within a week, he had moved out and while Larry still worried about Annie, who would spend alternate weeks with him, Jessica had indicated in their brief encounters over the past three years that things were better.

And while Jessica, Annie and Larry hardly had anything one could now call a relationship, since the incident, Jessica had made a point of dropping off the occasional meal for Larry with him reciprocating usually with treats for Annie.

Larry had suspected Jessica was hoping for something more with him, despite being at least 15-years younger than he was. But to her he was John Lawrence and any hope they might have for a relationship was trumped by Larry's need to stay anonymous.

Larry handed Jessica the bag of pepperettes. "For Annie."

Jessica looked in the bag. "Thanks, John, she'll love them."

There was an awkward silence. Larry wasn't sure whether it was because Jessica had made it clear she was alone or because of something else. He decided to ask. "Why are you surprised to see me?"

She looked at him for a moment. "Some cops came by the other day and then a detective. I think his name was Mason."

Larry kept his face impassive. "What were they looking for?"

"The cops weren't really looking for anything. Just asked if I had heard or seen anything on Monday morning, which I hadn't."

"And the detective?"

She frowned. "He asked about you and two other guys. I think one guy's name was Weathers, not sure of the other one."

Larry knew without asking that she would not have provided much to the detective. She didn't know very much and people these days didn't share more than they had to. Also, he knew Jessica was good people and cared about him.

After a few beats of silence. "John, is everything okay?"

"It's fine. Jess, thank you." He then gave her a quick kiss on the cheek. "I have to go, but I may stop by again later if that's okay." He said the last part for two reasons: first, he might really stop by later; and second, he couldn't think of any other way to end the conversation.

She touched her cheek. "Okay, John."

Less than a minute later, Larry reached the third floor landing. He knelt down against the wall next to his door and took his pocket knife out of his pocket.

Larry used the screwdriver on the knife to remove a faceplate at the base of the wall next to his door. There were several wires, but Larry knew what he was looking for. He detached a thin blue wire and then put the faceplate back on, leaving the screws in only loosely.

Larry then stood up. He reached up and unscrewed the hall light and then removed his key card and passed it over the reader to the side of his front door.

The door beeped and opened. All interior doors had been converted to electronics after the Occupied Zone had been set up. In this way, the government always knew who was coming or going.

But the system was pretty crude – the product of setting something up in a hurry and Larry knew how to trick it. A simple bit of surgery on one wire and the central mainframe would have no idea he had just entered his apartment. Eventually, someone could match the entries and exits versus what got uploaded to the mainframe and figure out that something was amiss, but Larry was fairly certain John Lawrence would not be living here for too much longer.

Larry stood now in his apartment. He already knew from his conversation with Jessica that they had been in the apartment and found his hiding spot. Despite this, whoever had been in here – Mason he supposed – had tried to hide their presence, which was amateurish considering Mason had apparently asked everyone in the building about John Lawrence, Dan LaRussa and Carl Weathers.

Larry left the lights out and stayed clear of the window. He thought about leaving and making his way to the park, but he was fairly certain that he was safe for the night and he had missed sleeping in his bed, despite the fact it wasn't all that comfortable.

He ate the sliced turkey he had bought and then went into the bathroom. He placed his Sig and key card on the sink (he had left the Glock with Kennex) and brushed his teeth. He tried to make out his face in the mirror, but it was hard to make much out in the dim light that came from the window in the main room. He then slipped out of the bathroom and into bed. Sleep came quickly.

47

November 6th, 2023

Sacramento, California

"When do you think truth stopped mattering?"

Fred Pugliano stared at Governor Beachum for a couple of beats. Before he could answer, Bill Tanner weighed in. "I don't think it was a fine line where truth mattered one day and then stopped mattering the next, Governor. I think it just got greyer and greyer over the years until at some point, narrative mattered more than facts."

The three men sat in the governor's office. It was 10:30 at night and the vote would be held the next day. Jameson's had been flowing freely for the past hour.

Pugliano nodded his head. "I think we tolerated a lot of sweet little lies for a while and then the lies starting getting bigger. Maybe it was WMD in Gulf War two or the whole way they tried to make it seem that Sadaam had anything to do with 911." He paused. "That's when it seems like to me we started jumping the shark on truth."

Tanner now interrupted. "And let's be clear, it wasn't just them. Both sides played fast and loose with the truth. The notion that we can somehow pay of all of these entitlements when the population is rapidly aging and health care is getting more and more expensive and there are fewer and fewer workers to support it all is utter nonsense. But our side demonizes anyone who even tries to open up the discussion on the topic, which in my view is a different kind of lying."

Beachum frowned. "Maybe, but man, they are way better at lying than we are."

The three men shared a half-hearted laugh. Pugliano now weighed in. "There was a story the other day on the Fox website. Quoted a fucking Iranian cleric, who claimed that he had been approached by Joe Tynan back during the 2020 campaign. Claimed Tynan promised that if he won, things would be better between Iran and the US." Pugliano paused and took a drink.

"So this fuck nuts tells Fox this, which anyone in DHS or the CIA could debunk in a matter of minutes because it's not like Tynan could travel secretly to Iran to meet with some Sheik or whatever the fuck this guy is, and DHS and CIA don't know about it. So Fox gets this and runs it, which is its own sort of batshit crazy and pretty much the antithesis of the definition of responsible journalism." He paused again to drink.

"So this is bad enough because people go to the Fox News website and read it and believe it. But then, Champer sees it, because no one reads this shit more than that fuckin' ass hat and he tweets about it. The President of the Fucking United States of Fucking America tweets about a fucking story that is so patently ludicrous and could be disproven in minutes by his own fucking intelligence apparatus and now a lie becomes fact to millions of Americans." He paused and stared at his now empty glass. "Makes me fuckin' sad."

The three men sat silently for several seconds and then Beachum started giggling. It took him about 30-seconds to compose himself. ""Ass hat" was inspired, Freddie. Quite the Lieutenant Governor we have in this great state. "

Pugliano smiled. Tanner was refilling everyone's glass with two fingers of the scotch. "Just calling a spade a spade, Governor."

Beachum raised his glass. "I'll drink to that."

The three men clinked glasses. "And it's not just facts, when the fuck did we lose nuance?"

Beachum stared at Pugliano. He had heard his nuance argument before, but he knew when to let his Lieutenant go on. "How so?"

Pugliano sighed. "We used to be able to explain issues as something other than black and white. Yeah, America imports more than it exports, but we have a massive population relative to most other countries and we have a consumption per capita way above every other country. So there is more of us and each of us consumes a lot more on average, so, of course, we are going to import a lot more than we export."

"When did we start talking about trade?" Tanner was staring at the scotch in his glass as he asked the question.

"We're not. I'm just making a point about nuance. If I go out on the campaign trail and start railing about the trade balance and how unfair it is, the crowd gets worked up into a frenzy about it. But if I go out there and say, yeah, the trade balance looks unfair, but on a per capita basis, it's really not and oh by the way, the trade imbalance is keeping prices for TVs and iPhones really low, so you are actually benefitting, the crowd would fall asleep inside of a minute. Champer and his ilk figured out way before us that nuance is dead and that makes me sad. Real fuckin' sad."

Tanner stared off into space and said, "sadder than the lie thing?"

"Fuck you, Bill." They all laughed again.

"You ever see the movie *Sliding Doors*?" Beachum now spoke in a somewhat somber tone.

Tanner shook his head. "Is it good?"

"No, not really. But in it, the main character, who I think was played by Gwyneth Paltrow, basically has the chance to live an event in two ways - in the first, she makes her train in time and in the second, she just misses the train."

Pugliano nodded. "And?"

Beachum continued. "And that simple twist of fate - you make a light and catch the train versus you hit a red and miss it - had profound effects on your future and the future of humanity."

Tanner drained his glass and looked at Beachum. "So the world ends because she missed the train?"

Beachum smiled. "No, but by making the train, she catches her boyfriend cheating on her and kicks him out. Eventually, she lives happily ever after because of it."

Pugliano now looking interested, leaned in. "And when she misses it?"

"Her life turns to shit because she never catches him cheating and ends up staying with him."

Tanner rose to fill his glass again. "And you think this describes the world we live in today?"

Beachum made a face. "Sort of. Think of all the sliding doors moments we've had over the last 20-years."

As he poured, Tanner asked. "You mean the vote?"

Beachum shook his head. "The vote is only the latest and arguably the outcomes of a yes vote and no vote may not be all that different. I'm thinking about Champer. What if Obama never roasts him at the Correspondents dinner or what if NBC shoots down his TV show, which apparently it almost did? Something like that."

They all sat there in thought for a moment. Beachum then continued. "Did you know he tried to buy a football team and the NFL wouldn't let him?"

Pugliano nodded. "I seem to remember something like that. The Browns or maybe it was the Bills."

Beachum shrugged. "It doesn't matter - but that was a sliding doors moment - he buys that team and everything is probably different - he doesn't go the TV personality route and he doesn't become a birther and he doesn't get roasted and he doesn't run, and, and, and."

Tanner stared at Beachum for several seconds and then said, "so the NFL fucked us all?"

Beachum smiled. "In a matter of speaking."

They all sat in silence for a few minutes and then turned their attention to the television, which was tuned to CNN.

"What are the polls telling us, Jeffrey?" CNN anchor Storm Masters turned to CNN's political expert, Jeff Harrison.

"The polling aggregates suggest that this is going to be a close call, Storm. While most Californians support Governor Beachum, in fact, by an overwhelming 71%; the secession vote is currently polling at only 43% yes, 41% with still roughly 15% undecided."

Tanner muted the television. "Going to be exciting."

The room got quiet for a moment and then Tanner spoke again. "Seriously, George – what's your gut, ummm, what are your thoughts on all this?"

Beachum stared at Tanner for a few beats. "My gut tells me nothing at this point. But I will say this for posterity …"

Tanner felt his pockets as though looking for pen. "Sorry, left my pen on my desk."

Beachum rolled his eyes and continued. "I will say this, if we win, I think the first thing we do is offer an olive branch to Champer. Let's sit down and work this out. In other words, I think the vote is only the first step, not the final step."

"Like with Brexit."

"Exactly, Freddie. There is a certain irony that the President who championed Brexit when the Brits went down this road is now getting hit with Calzit or whatever the hell they are calling it."

"Calexit," added Pugliano.

"Anyway, if we win, I think we go that route. Maybe I'm being naïve or trying to use nuance, but maybe it takes something like this to shake the tree and get them to meet us in the middle."

"And if we lose?" Asked Tanner.

Beachum paused and then smiled. "We all hide behind Freddie." They all laughed again.

A moment later, Beachum's phone buzzed. He looked at the phone and then at Pugliano and Tanner. "It's Katie."

Beachum put the call on speaker phone. "Hey sweetie."

"Daddy? How are you holding up?"

Beachum smiled. "Good, honey. I'm here with Freddie and Bill. They were just regaling me with tails of adventure."

Tanner said, "Hey Kates!", while Pugliano added, "hey slugger!"

"Daddy, I'm going to get on a plane and come home."

Beachum made a face. "I don't think that would be a good idea. There's a lot going on over here and I don't want you in harm's way."

"Daddy, I am 22-years old, I have spent the past four years in ROTC. I can take care of myself."

"I know you can. But I prefer you buttoned up in England rather than dealing with the bullshit over here. As soon as this is over, we will talk about bringing you home."

There was silence from the phone for a few beats. "Dad, take me off speaker."

Beachum picked up the phone and switched to handset. "It's off."

Beachum listened to the phone for almost a minute and then spoke. "It's not going to come to that, Kate."

Beachum then listened to the phone again for roughly fifteen seconds and then said, "I love you too, honey. And Katie, you take care."

Beachum clicked off and stared back at Tanner and Pugliano. Tears had begun to streak down his cheeks.

Pugliano handed him a tissue. "You okay, boss?"

Beachum took the tissue and stared off into space unsure or the first time of whether he would see his little girl again.

48

July 1st, 2034

Los Angeles, California

Mason parked the 2028 Ford Phoenix in front of 212 Reardon. Murphy looked around the street as Mason grabbed his door handle.

"Wait, Mark. Let's just get a sense of things before we go in."

Mason exhaled. He had heard Murphy's laws repeatedly over the past five years. The fifth law or was it the sixth was – get a sense for your surroundings.

After about a minute, Murphy grabbed his door handle. "Okay, let's check it out."

Mason had called Murphy at home. They had not gotten a hit on Lawrence's apartment, but Jessica Rosen, who lived right below Lawrence had had a visitor.

Mason had identified her as a person of interest. When he had questioned her about Lawrence and the other identities, she had seemed a bit uncomfortable – like she knew Lawrence better than she let on. Could be a romantic thing as she was roughly the right age and very pleasing to look at.

Murphy stood on the street and took another look around. It was about 10:30 PM and there was not surprisingly no one to be seen given the curfew.

Mason keyed in to his phone. "Detectives Mason and Murphy on camera 474."

"Copy, 474," said the dispatcher's voice.

Mason nodded at Murphy and the two men walked into 212. It was Murphy's first time in the building and the foyer struck him as the very essence of the shitty world they now lived in. There was no furniture and the lights were dimmer than they should be, giving the room a desolate feel.

After doing another quick check of the surroundings, Murphy walked to the stairs and the two detectives walked up to the second floor. Murphy stopped at apartment 21. He looked at Mason.

Mason whispered. "Do we stop here first?"

Murphy stared at him and shook his head. "Let's go up. I want to see Lawrence's place first. She's not going anywhere."

Mason nodded and they walked up to the third floor. The light in the hall was out. Murphy immediately drew his .38.

Mason looked at him unsure of what was happening. Murphy pointed to the light and held his fingers to his lips. There was enough light coming up from the second floor and down from the fourth for Murphy and Mason to see, but the shadows were long. Mason drew his .357 cannon as he liked to call it.

Mason nodded. Murphy took out his pocket flashlight and quickly scanned the door and the rest of the third floor landing. No sounds or signs were evident.

Murphy stood there in the dark, unsure of what to do. They could call in a ram team and do this the proper way, but it was possible the light was simply out or that Lawrence had come and gone.

He looked at Mason. Get on the phone and have command check on traffic into and out of ..." he paused and shined the light on Lawrence's door. "32".

Mason keyed his phone and whispered. "Dispatch?"

"Copy."

"Any traffic today on 212 Reardon, apartment 32, over."

"Copy, 212 Reardon, apartment 32, over." After about ten seconds. "Negative, over."

Murphy stood there in thought. "Have them open it."

Mason keyed his phone again. "Dispatch, open 212 Reardon, apartment 32, over."

"Copy. Opening 212 Reardon, apartment 32, over."

Murphy and Mason stood in the dark waiting for the distinctive click of the door opening. After about 20-seconds, Mason clicked his phone again.

"Dispatch, have you activated the door, over?"

"Copy, door at 212 Reardon, apartment 32 has been activated, over."

"Fuck, fuck, fuck," Murphy whispered.

"I say we kick the fucker in."

Murphy did not acknowledge Mason's statement. He thought about what Emma had said to him earlier in the night. How did he want this to end?

Mason then said, "I'm going in."

Murphy tried to reach for Mason, but he kicked the door hard. It did not open on the first kick, but gave on the second.

49

November 4th, 2020

Washington, District of Columbia

"Fox News now projects that once again, President Richard Harrison Champer has proven the polls wrong and he will remain the President of the United States for another term."

Dimitri sat alone in his hotel room. He raised a glass of vodka to the screen and took a large swallow.

The phone was ringing. It would be President Popov wishing to congratulate him. Dimitri stared at the phone and decided not to answer it. He was enjoying the moment and he did not feel like being sycophantic at that moment.

The night had been closer than he had thought, pushing well past midnight. While a couple of states were still too close to call – New Hampshire and surprisingly Iowa - Champer would win somewhere in the range of 275 to 285 electoral votes, barely above the 270 needed for reelection.

Dimitri stared at the screen, which he had muted, at the large smiling face of Champer and the checkmark beneath it.

Dimitri took another drink. The next four years held so much promise for the Motherland.

50

July 1st, 2034

Los Angeles, California

The first kick woke Larry out of a deep sleep. He instinctively rolled to the floor between the bed and the window. He reached under the bedspring and realized at that moment that the Sig was in the bathroom.

A second kick opened the door. No one entered at first and then Larry saw the shape of a man move into the room.

"Mark, fuck. Dammit." A man standing outside the door whispered.

Larry kept low. The light from the window behind him would make him visible. The two men were now in the room.

"Lawrence, LAPD. We know you are in here. Come on out and no one gets hurt."

Larry lay on the floor. His mind was quickly working out various permutations and combinations. He was fairly certain these guys were cops – no one actually declared themselves to be cops if they weren't. He just wasn't sure how trigger happy they were.

He stood up. "Easy there, officer."

The man reflexively fired. The bullet whizzed by Larry's shoulder. He could feel the rush. Without hesitating, he ducked low and bull rushed the man plowing him into the second man, who was standing behind him. The three ended up in a pile by the door.

Larry thrust his fist into the shooter's neck. He instantly began to gag and struggle for breath. The second man, who was laying flat on his back, but was out of Larry's reach, still held his gun and started to bring it around.

Larry picked up the discarded gun from the man he had incapacitated and placed it against the groin of the other man.

"Not a good idea."

The man looked down at the gun and let go of his own.

"Oh, for fuck sake." The prone man muttered.

Larry stood up and grabbed the gagging man by the foot, dragging him into the room, while keeping the gun on the other man. The other man got up and crawled into the room, the semi-splintered down shutting behind him.

Larry sat on the bed, gun pointed at the one man. The other continued to gag. He was breathing, but his larynx was partially crushed and he would need some serious help – soon.

"You police?"

Murphy stared at him. "Yes. I'm detective Sam Murphy and this is detective Mark Mason."

Larry looked at Murphy. "Okay, detective Murphy. Let's start with you getting on the phone and signaling the all clear."

Murphy stared at Larry. He then pointed at Mason. "He's got the phone." Larry nodded and Murphy reached across Mason's prone body for his phone.

"Dispatch, all clear at 212 Reardon, apartment 32, over."

"Copy, all clear, over."

Murphy looked at Larry. "Someone's going to report the gunshot, John."

Larry stared at Murphy. He was unclear why Murphy appeared to be helping him. "Fair enough, give me the quick 60 seconds on what you know."

Murphy squinted in the dark. He had no doubt Lawrence would kill him if he tried anything. The way he had quickly disarmed the two men was professional and while he would not testify to it in a court of law, he was fairly certain Lawrence had dodged the bullet Mason had fired.

"Ummm, we don't really know very much. Whoever the hell you are, you have done a pretty bang up job of staying off the grid. Mark here," he pointed at Mason, who had passed out, "did some detective work and figured out that you were somehow involved in a shooting the other night. That caused him to search your place and find the IDs and the tac gear."

"And why are you here now?"

Murphy did not hesitate. "Because you visited the girl downstairs on your way in tonight. We had tagged her as a person of interest in this whole thing."

"She okay?"

"We didn't even stop in to see her."

Larry stared at Murphy. It was moment of truth time. "How much have you called in tonight, detective Murphy?"

Murphy stared at the shape of what he thought of as John Lawrence. He could not make out the man's face, but his tone worried him. "Nothing. Just getting clearance and opening your door."

Larry bit his lip. There was no pleasant way for this to end.

"I'm sorry, Sam, you don't deserve this."

Larry shot Murphy in the chest with Mason's .357. He fell back. On his way out, he grabbed the Sig, threw his remaining clothes in a bag and left the apartment for the last time.

On the way down, he stopped at apartment 21. Jessica answered almost immediately. "John, I heard the shots, what is happening?"

Larry was cold and ruthless, but not that cold and ruthless. "Jess, some stuff is going to come down over the next few days. You don't owe me anything, but I just wanted you to know that I'm sorry."

She stared at Larry, tears forming in her eyes. "I would never do anything that could get you into trouble. I, ummm, I ..."

Larry shook his head. "Don't" and then, "I know." He paused. "Take care of Annie." He kissed her on the lips and lingered for a moment.

"Wait three minutes and then call in and report the gunshots."

She watched as he disappeared down the stairs.

Upstairs in apartment 32, Detective Sam Murphy struggled to breath. The Kevlar vest that he wore had absorbed the bullet, but he was sure multiple ribs were at the very least cracked and potentially broken.

Lawrence had to know that all cops wore vests at all times. The technology had advanced to the point that vests were barely noticeable and could stop almost anything.

He turned his head and looked at Mason, who was still unconscious. He moved his hand around the floor until it closed on Mark's phone. He passed out before he could put in the call to dispatch.

51

July 1st, 2034

Los Angeles, California

Fifteen minutes later, Larry sat in the same copse of trees in Klein Park. He had passed two patrols on the way to the park, but he had only heard sirens when he was arriving in the park, meaning the cops likely were not on his trail.

He felt bad about shooting Murphy. He could tell even in the dark that he was wearing Kevlar, had felt it when he tackled his and the other detective. But the .357 was powerful and with Murphy's age, Larry figured he was over 60, and at such close range, it was not out of the realm of possibility that the shot had killed him. Regardless, assuming he survived, he was going to be out of commission for a while.

As for Mason, Larry was confident he would survive, but again, he was going to be in recovery for a long time with a chance that his career was over – throats were a fragile thing as an old colleague used to say.

Larry inventoried what he had. He now had three guns with him – the Sig he had purchased a couple of days earlier, Mason's .357 and Murphy's .38. He had a few changes of clothes, a bit of cash, his ration card, his pocket knife and not much else. He could survive for a while, but he had basically reached a crossroads.

He had hidden in plain sight for five-years. He could now go on the run, get out of the Occupied Zone and then figure it out in Free America. While the cops still probably had no idea who he was, if they spent enough time going through the camera footage of the area around Reardon, they might get a pretty good idea of what John Lawrence actually looked like. He doubted Murphy got much of a look in the dark and Mason certainly didn't, but the gestapo could have him in a week or two.

The red pill, as Larry liked to call it, told him to stay. While he had yet to hear the FOB plan for the docks, he suspected it would all set into motion in the next week. It was risky as the cops may figure out who he was before it all came down, but Larry's gut told him that he would probably be okay.

And he liked the idea of the red pill. He had spent five-years hiding and while there were obviously good reasons to stay hidden, the bitter memory of Beth weighed on him every day.

Also, there was Karen or whatever her name was. He had spent only a few hours with her, but save for the kiss he had just planted on Jessica's lips, it was the most intimate he'd been with a woman since Beth.

Larry put his stuff back into the bag and sat down against a tree. He closed his eyes – he had decided to take the red pill one more time.

52

November 7ᵗʰ, 2023

Washington, District of Columbia

"Breaking news, CNN now projects that the state of California will support secession."

The Cabinet Room was silent. CNN anchor, Storm Masters continued, "the issue that has hung over this country for months has now been resolved. With 68% of precincts reporting, the yes votes are running nearly 20% ahead of the no votes, a much wider margin, I repeat, a much wider margin than expected. Let's now turn to our CNN panel of experts to get a sense for what this means."

Someone, Champer wasn't sure who, muted the television. He sat there in silence. He then said calmly and coldly, "Cal, I thought you said it was a coin flip."

Doggett stared at the President. "All of our polling suggested it would be close, sir." He paused checking the legal pad in front of him. "It looks like it broke late."

Champer smiled. "It broke late. Yes, it broke late." He stared down at the conference room table and then, "clear the room please, Cal, Pete, you stay."

The various cabinet secretaries and White House staff shuffled out of the room. Champer kept a cool smile on his face, raising his chin and giving some of the more upset folks a thumbs up.

After the room had cleared. "Okay, take me through it."

Doggett looked at Partridge, who nodded. He was a three-star and he felt like a little kid. "United Coast is ready to go, sir."

"When?"

Doggett looked at Partridge. "Mr. President, I think we should reconsider this."

Champer turned to Partridge. "Reconsider what, Pete?"

He cleared his throat. "Sir, we lost. History can remember this one way or history can remember it another. I think we pick up the phone and call Beachum and we extend an olive branch."

"Extend an olive branch?"

"Yes, sir. Beachum is a pragmatist. Hell, in a former life, he and I were even friends. He knows that secession is a nightmare for California. I mean, are they going to default on all their debts now? Are they going to issue their own currency? And while the vote went against us, there were still more than five million people who cast votes against secession. How is he going to deal with them?"

The room was silent.

After about a minute. "Cal?"

Doggett looked at the President. "Yes, sir?"

"What do you think of what he said?" He pointed his thumb at Partridge without looking at him.

"I think .." just then, the phone on the table rang.

Champer looked at the phone and then at Doggett and nodded.

Doggett pressed one of the buttons in front of him on the table. "Go ahead."

"Sirs, we have George Beachum on the phone."

Champer looked at Doggett and nodded again. "Put him through please, Shirley."

Champer said. "Hello, George. What can we do for you?"

"Mr. President, thank you for taking my call." Beachum's voice was raspy. There had clearly been some celebrating going on at his end.

"Thank you for calling me, George. I have the Vice President and General Doggett here with me."

"Mr. Vice President, General." Beachum insisted on the formalities. "I am assuming you have seen the results of the vote?"

Champer kept an even demeanor. "We have, George."

Beachum cleared his throat. "Mr. President, we don't want this to run its course, but we will if we have to. The people of California have spoken, but I think cooler heads can still prevail."

Champer raised his eyebrows and looked at Doggett and Partridge. "Go on?"

"Yes, Mr. President. I would like to propose that we sit down and start a dialogue. I think there is a middle ground here that keeps the largest state in the country as part of this great Union. A win/win if you would allow, Mr. President."

Champer smiled. "I like your style, George."

"Thank you, Mr. President."

"Okay, we will meet. And given the issues and risks to you, I will come there if that's okay, George."

Beachum paused. "Ummm, of course, Mr. President. We'd like that, sir."

"Great, my people and your people will get it figured out."

"Thank you, Mr. President."

Champer replied. "No, thank you, George." He then clicked off the line.

Champer sat back and looked at Doggett and Partridge. He continued to smile. "Cal, I want a meeting tonight of the Joint Chiefs."

Doggett nodded. "Yes, sir."

He turned to Partridge. "Pete, I want your resignation before you leave this room."

Champer stood up and walked out. Doggett and Partridge continued to stare at one another well after Champer had left the room.

53

November 7th, 2023

Sacramento, California

The President hung up. Beachum looked at Tanner. "Holy shit."

Tanner tried to rub the cobwebs from his eyes from champagne they had been drinking. The two men were alone aside from Beachum's head of security. "I have to admit, Governor. I didn't see it going quite that way."

Beachum had come to rely on Tanner's ability to see the chess board. "Not every day someone surprises Big Bill Tanner."

Tanner laughed, but was staring off into space. "No sir, it isn't."

The revelry from the other side of the door continued. Despite boldly going where no state had gone since the 1860s, Beachum's staff was going to have at least one night of celebration.

"So we meet and negotiate and maybe this is what gets us back on the righteous path."

Tanner now focused on Beachum. "I guess so. Man, I did not see him reacting that way. Maybe he has finally been humbled by it all." He said the last part as more of a question than as a statement.

Beachum sat back. "He has just lost the biggest state in the Union and the fifth largest economy in the world. He's got New York, New Jersey and a bunch of other states lining up to do the same. He's got a stock market crash and an economy that has been stumbling for the better part of three years. He's got Russia advancing on Europe. He's got a shit-storm pretty much everywhere you look. Even a complete lunatic is going to be humbled by that."

Tanner stared again off into space and then focused again on Beachum. "When you put it that way. Yes, it makes sense."

"Okay, so we announce that we are going to meet here in California with Champer and negotiate terms so to speak."

Tanner interrupted. "You realize that there's a good chance he changes his mind. I mean, his M.O. is to tweet the opposite of what he just said."

Beachum sighed. "That's fair, but let's at least give it a chance."

After about 30-seconds of silence. "I agree, sir. We make an announcement and prepare for a meeting."

The two men sat back and returned to their silence. After about 15-seconds, Beachum's head of security cleared his throat.

Beachum looked up. "You have something you'd like to say?"

His head of security looked down and then back at Beachum. "Sir, my gut tells me that this is a trap."

Beachum looked at Tanner, who raised his eyebrows and then Beachum turned back. "Go on, Larry."

54

April 11th, 2013

Southern Mediterranean Sea

Larry dove out of the small boat and surfaced about 30-feet later. They had discussed his wearing scuba gear and going in sub-surface the whole way, but it was dark and Larry was a powerful swimmer and they had decided it would be cleaner to go in sans the scuba gear.

While the current in the Med was against him as he swam to the shore of the small private island, Larry's powerful stroke easily cut through the water.

Seven minutes later, Larry reached the shore. He removed his night vision goggles from his pack and did a quick scan of the beach. There was no moonlight, and he was virtually invisible amongst the rocks that dotted the shore.

Larry then inserted his ear piece. "Copy."

"This is mother, we got you, Red Bear." Replied Malcolm's gravelly voice. "The drone has you five by five, over. We sight zero bogies in your vicinity, over."

"Copy, mother."

Larry advanced up the beach and reached the tree-line. Through the trees about 50-meters ahead he could see the lights of the mansion.

"Red Bear, we have four bogies positioned about ten meters apart around the back edge of the compound, over."

"Copy, mother."

They had dropped Larry at the backside of the island as the approach was easier. The front side had pronounced cliffs and a stronger current, which would have made swimming in nearly impossible.

Larry moved carefully through the trees. The area wasn't quite jungle, but it was still thick. He wore a black thermal protected diving suit, which offered all the protection he needed from any stray branches. It also had the added benefit of shielding his heat signature in case anyone in the compound had infrared. He tread carefully as they were not sure whether any trip wire had been set. He doubted it given thickness of the brush, but one could never be too careful.

After about three minutes of making his way through the brush. Larry squatted and sighted the back of the compound.

"Mother, I'm in position alpha."

After about ten seconds, Malcolm responded. "You are a go, Red Bear."

"Copy, mother." Larry removed his silenced .300 caliber Winchester M2020 from his shoulder and sited the four targets.

He then called out, "foxtrot one, confirmed. Foxtrot two, confirmed, Foxtrot three, confirmed. Foxtrot four, confirmed."

Malcolm responded. "Red Bear, I have four confirmed down, over. No other exterior bogies, over."

Larry broke into a run and reached the perimeter of the compound in 20-seconds. He ran to the right side of the large swimming pool and stopped at a staircase at the back of the house that led to the basement.

"I've reached position beta. Going down."

"Copy that, Red Bear. Good luck and God speed."

Larry did not acknowledge the good wishes. He was now going to be inside the house of one of the most notorious terrorists in North Africa. They had decided that he would go radio silent when inside as they were unsure how the technology inside the house would react to their equipment.

Larry activated the timer on his watch. He had 90 seconds. He had slung the M2020 over his shoulder and he drew his trusty Glock, which was also silenced. Thermal scans told them that there were at least ten men inside, including Anwar Assan.

Assan was not your traditional terrorist, but rather the biggest sponsor of piracy in the Mediterranean. Over the past six-years, Assan's organization had been responsible for the deaths of 116 people and had stolen hundreds of millions, perhaps even billions, in cargo.

Larry moved quickly through the basement. He turned at a large wine cellar and approached the stairs leading up to the first level. He checked his watch – 25 seconds had elapsed.

Larry crouched and move quickly up the stairs. Their intel told them that the basement door opened onto the kitchen. Larry reached the door and with his left hand turned the handle and edged it open. A maid was in the kitchen with her back to the basement door. Larry edged into the room and then moved quickly down a hallway. He could hear voices from what they thought was the living room.

He reached the front foyer of the house, his back against the wall that opened into the living room. A large well-lit staircase led to the second level. He took a breath and rounded into the room.

Three men sat on a large sectional, while another sat in a chair. They were all watching a soccer match. Larry shot them all between the eyes – the three of them never even saw him.

Larry pivoted out of the room and headed up the stairs. None of the men had been Assan. His watch vibrated – it had already been 90 seconds.

Larry reached the top of the stairs. A moment later an alarm began to blare. The men outside had not checked in as they were supposed to every two minutes. Someone in the control room, which was located just next to where Larry now stood had hit the alarm.

Larry kicked open the door and started firing. Three shots were wildly fired back at him, but Larry continued firing, emptying his clip into the three men that now lay dead. None of the bullets they had fired at him had come close.

Larry slapped a fresh clip into the Glock and turned and ran toward Assan's bedroom. The alarm had been sounded about ten seconds before and that coupled with the roars of the un-silenced weapons of Assan's men would have surely roused Assan.

Larry never slowed and threw his shoulder into Assan's bedroom door and then immediately rolled to the floor. Assan, dressed in only pajama pants, was halfway into his closet, which was also a safe room. He had a gun in his left hand. A naked woman was screaming on the bed.

Larry fired twice, hitting Assan in the thigh and in the chest. He then stood up and shot Assan between the eyes.

Larry stared at the body for a moment and then a roar filled the room. Larry hit the wall next to the door, his left arm and chest burning. He turned and fired twice, hitting the naked woman in the right cheek and the forehead.

Larry fell to the ground, the shot had knocked the wind out of him; although, from what he could tell, his left arm just below the shoulder had absorbed most of the damage.

Larry rose and looked at the woman. Her death made nine. The maid was the only one left alive in the house besides Larry and he wasn't going to kill her unless he had to.

Larry stumbled down the stairs. His arm was on fire. He rounded the corner and came face to face with the maid. She stood there frozen in the kitchen. Larry held the Glock low, but she seemed more scared than a threat. He nodded to her as he exited through the back kitchen door.

Five minutes later Larry reached the beach. He had lost a fair bit of blood and was gradually losing consciousness.

"Mother, come in."

Malcolm responded, "Go ahead, Red Bear."

"Target confirmed. Going to need an assisted evac, over."

"Copy, evac inbound."

Fourteen minutes later, Larry sat in state room on the large yacht that Malcolm had somehow commandeered. His arm was wrapped and he was drinking a glass of water. He sat back, the image of the dead woman burned in his mind.

"You okay?" Angus "Daxx" Daxton had peaked his head in. Larry had recruited him the year before to join the team.

"I'll live, Daxx."

"Okay, let me know if you need anything. And Red Bear .."

"Yeah?"

"Nice fucking work."

Daxx left and Larry lay back. The phone in his pocket buzzed. It was an incoming text.

Larry, beginning to fade from the loss of blood and the events of the evening, pulled the phone close to his face and squinted to read the text.

"Hey Larry, its Beth Jennings. Long time, no talk. 4 yrs – wow. Was at that Mexican restaurant we used to eat at all the time. The one with the chocolate tacos for desert. Anywell, I got to thinking about you and us and"

Larry waited. The second text came about a minute later. Larry had actually briefly passed out when the buzzing returned.

"Stupid text message. Anyway, I got to thinking about us and I miss us, Larry. I miss you. Anyway, call me if this isn't completely crazy."

Larry lowered the phone and laid back. As he faded out, he thought of Beth Jennings.

55

November 25th, 2023

Alabaster, Alabama

James "Jimmy" Bienemy sipped his coffee. Greta had a way of making the coffee that was a bit less acrid than Hazel, the other waitress at Dick's Diner, so Jimmy preferred to come to Dick's on Mondays, Wednesdays and Saturdays when he had figured out that Greta was on coffee duty.

"The usual, Jimmy?" Greta gave Jimmy a wink. Even though she knew Jimmy was happily married, Jimmy wasn't hard to look at and he was a good tipper for a regular.

Jimmy blushed a bit. He would never think of cheating on Barb, but he had to admit it wasn't just the coffee that brought him to Dick's. "Yes, maam." His response was delivered a bit sheepishly and with his head tilted down as he sometimes struggled to make eye contact with Greta.

Most at the counter at the diner had their heads pointed up and to the left, focused on the television, which was tuned to Fox & Friends.

"Can you turn it up, Greta?" Chris Meadows, who ran the Domtar paper mill here in Vance was parked at his usual corner spot at the counter.

Greta grabbed the remote and unmuted the television.

"What's the bigger surprise here, Judge? Is it Vice President Partridge abruptly resigning or President Champer potentially choosing his own son to replace him?"

Judge Janice Tenudo sat back and observed her co-host. Tenudo had only actually been a judge for two years of her 40+ year legal career. Despite this, she was frequently rumored to be a potential choice for a Federal appeals court or even in some circles – a US Supreme Court seat. It was well known that she had Champer's ear, so she made a point of choosing her words carefully.

"I don't think the Vice President had much choice here, Annie. He and the President had clearly been at odds over the past few months with the VP seemingly more interested in the 2024 campaign than in helping President Champer to govern through some very challenging times." Tenudo paused. "And that was before California and New York effectively declared war on this great country."

Bienemy, who had been focused on his eggs, looked up. He liked Champer, at least his no bullshit attitude, but what Tenudo had just said was its own sort of bullshit. Everyone knew that the Vice President had helped to push the abortion law over the line. Beinemy was certain he had heard Judge Janice trumpet such on this show only a few weeks before.

"And what about the rumors that Dick Jr. could be his choice to replace the Vice President?" Annie Walters, who was less of a cohost and more of the "straight man" for Judge Janice tried to sound official with her question, putting her pen up to her lips as she finished.

Tenudo nodded her head. "I think it would be a brilliant choice and one likely to be supported not only by the people of this country — at least those not living in elitist enclaves — but also by the House and the Senate. And with Democratic Senator Harkens currently hospitalized and unable to cast a vote, the President should act quickly as he doesn't have the VP to cast the tie-breaking vote anymore."

"I hadn't thought of that, Judge Janice." She paused as if searching for her next question. "Quickly as we have to go to commercial, but I have to ask you about the California vote and the fact that the President has agreed to go to California to try to resolve this. Do you think this is a sign of weakness on his part?"

Bienemy noticed that the diner was now completely quiet. Everyone was now focused on the television and Judge Janice's response to Walters' question.

Alabaster, Alabama, which was a small suburb of Birmingham, was the very definition of Champer country. He had carried the county by 31 points in 2016 and by 37 in 2020. While most in the county struggled a bit with Champer's hard edges (the churches were always full on Sundays), they appreciated his approach to immigration and trade and his love for the country.

Judge Janice looked at the camera. It almost seemed to Jimmy as if she was talking directly to the President. "I think he has to be careful not to show any weakness, Annie. What the liberal elites are doing is nothing short of high treason. Some would argue, and I'm not saying I agree with this, that Champer would be in his rights to have Beachum and his flunkies imprisoned and tried for high crimes. As many viewers probably know, high crimes carry the death penalty."

Bienemy stared at the television. He was pretty sure Judge Janice had not answered the question. He didn't like what California was doing any more than the next guy, but he also didn't like where this was all heading.

He asked Greta for the check, dropped $10 on the counter and walked out.

56

December 14th, 2023

Sacramento, California

"So they handle all logistics?"

Larry nodded at Daxton. "Secret Service has jurisdiction over all matters involving the President."

Larry stood at the head of the boardroom table. Around the table were the ten men who would be assigned to Governor Beachum's security detail for the President's visit in two days' time.

"So we just allow the Governor to go in there with a bunch of Champer's armed guards and hope for the best?" Derek "Deke" Dawkins, who was a former Army Ranger, looked skeptically at Larry.

Larry looked down at his notes. Larry had run Beachum's security detail for close to four-years. When he had left the CIA, he had bounced around a bit, uncertain of what he wanted to do. With the marriage to Beth and with the kids, he didn't want to put himself out there too far anymore.

Beachum's number two, Bill Tanner, had reached out to Larry after getting his name from his old CO – Jim Davies. Tanner had been concerned about the Governor's security in the post-Champer world, especially since Beachum seemed to revel so much in giving it to Champer as good as he got.

Larry had reached out to some of his old buddies in the CIA, who had hooked him up with some guys in the Secret Service.

Larry had wanted to know what he might be getting himself into before joining Beachum's security detail. They had laid out for him that protection was less about tactics and more about logistics. That is – if you made sure you crossed all your t's and fully planned out every appearance down to the last detail, including sending advance teams, restricting the use of electronics, etcetera – you essentially mitigated 99% of all potential threats.

Larry's whole career had been spent on the planning phase. To be sure - he had to improvise on a number of occasions as all situations could experience an "unknown factor" as Mastrianni used to call them (Mastrianni was Malcolm Mastrianni, who had been Larry's CIA recruiter and eventually his copilot on most missions) – but he had rarely, if ever, gone into a situation without having a strong grasp of the known factors.

Thus, he saw the security detail as an opportunity to continue his craft, but without the constant worry of whether the next mission might be his last.

And until the past few months, the job had pretty much been everything he might have hoped. Beachum got a fair number of death threats and they spent some time in front of some hostile crowds and in some sketchy areas, but Larry had assembled a strong team – he had insisted on having full logistics control when he took the job, including all manpower decisions – and he had ingrained in them the importance of planning.

The past few months had been different, however. The world had already become a much scarier place with the vitriol on both sides reaching a fever pitch. And then Beachum had made his announcement and the world had unraveled even more.

Larry, who had come to rely on his gut over the years, practically had an ulcer from the number of times his gut had warned him of something over the past six-months.

He now looked up and focused on what Dawkins had said. "No, we plan everything down to the last detail and then we hope for the best."

They all laughed. Larry was not sure he was kidding. "Rusty, why don't you gives us a status update?"

Randall "Rusty" Russo stroked his greying beard. "Secret Service and the marines came in last week. They have removed all electronics from the conference room where the meeting will take place and put in their own. The Black Hawk guys came down yesterday. Aside from looking menacing and all "tatted up", they have mostly stayed out of the way."

Larry turned to Daxton. He realized as he looked at the man that they had now worked together for most of the past 15-years. "Angus, what can you tell us about Black Hawk?"

Daxton frowned. "A real bunch of motherfuckers. Champer as we well know wasn't satisfied with traditional security, so just after the 2020 Election, he decided to augment his Secret Service detail with a bunch of the private contractors. Black Hawk employs the biggest, baddest looking hombres, so not surprising he went with them. Thus far, they have generally stood around and look menacing, but they have roughed up a few folks at some speeches, which I guess has proven Champer's point, because no one really protests at his speeches anymore for fear of getting knocked around by Black Hawk."

He turned back to Russo. "Rusty, who's in the room?" Even though Larry knew all the answers, he would insist on his team going over everything.

"Champer and his son, I mean the VP. And Governor Beachum and Mr. Tanner on the other side of the table. The President will have four Secret Service in there and they have agreed that you can be in there, boss." He paused.

"Outside the room is a bit unclear. There are likely to be about ten Secret Service and probably three or four of the Black Hawk guys in the governor's office, as well as me, Daxx, Wes and Crombie. There will also be some aides from both sides, but again, we don't have enough information to know who at this point."

"And outside?"

"The marines will take up station outside, as will the rest of our security detail. We will have all three teams on site, so it is going to be pretty crowded."

"And tense."

"Yeah, boss. Tense as a motherfucker."

57

July 2nd, 2034

Los Angeles, California

Larry sat in the living room of 14 Wesson, sipping a glass of water. He had just filled in Kennex, Karen, Ken Dougherty and Cory Nelson about the events of the night before.

Larry had worried that his day at work might be interrupted by a visit from the gestapo. The visit never came, while Larry passed easily through all checkpoints. The news had spent the better part of the last 12-hours focused on the events at 212 Reardon and it would not be long until they had a basic description of the man who resided in apartment 32.

Larry had been very careful over the years with the cameras on and around Reardon. He was fairly certain that while his image with on the mainframe hundreds, maybe thousands of times, it would not be easy to figure out that the guy caught on the images was the same guy that resided in 32.

Detectives Mason and Murphy were both expected to survive. State TV had described them both in stable condition. Larry doubted if either would be able to provide much of a description other than – the guy in 32 really kicked our asses.

That said – the gestapo would figure it out eventually.

Larry had decided his only choice was to go back to 14 Wesson and to fill them in on everything that had happened.

Karen sat back and looked at Kennex, who sat in the chair next to her. Dougherty and Nelson stood behind them. "What do you think?"

Kennex bit his lower lip as if in thought. "I think we go in two days as planned. As Larry laid out, they probably have no idea who he is and they won't before the Fourth. The delivery is set to come in that morning and Larry, Ken, Cory and I can go over all the details tomorrow night on what needs to be done."

Kennex paused and rubbed two of his fingers together. Karen had noticed over the years this was a nervous tick of his. "Champer's team has now officially announced his Fourth of July schedule and the docks are a part of it. Is it possible they change it up because of Reardon? I doubt it, so unless we run into the buzz saw of really good detective work, I think we're good."

Karen nodded. "I agree. But with one caveat."

All eyes in the room focused on her. "Larry, you give us the whole story of who you really are."

Larry looked at Karen for several beats and then looked down. He had figured this was coming. Again, his gut was almost never wrong.

He looked at her again and then at the three men in the room. He then looked down again. Had it really been eleven years?

"I killed the President."

The room sat silent for 30-seconds. And then Kennex spoke. "You're Larry Nash?"

End Part 2

58

December 16th. 2023

Sacramento, California

They were already behind schedule. The President's motorcade was supposed to arrive at 10 AM PST, but it was already nearly 10:45 and there were no signs of them.

Larry stood by the front door of the Governor's mansion once again checking in with his various team leaders. His gut was flashing red, but his team was only seeing their calm and cool leader at work.

He looked across the lawn of the compound. Roughly 15 marines milled about in no particular formation, while another smaller group monitored the various surveillance drones that were circling above

"We have them."

It was Liam Zassner, Larry's number three, who was stationed by the guard booth 200-meters outside the compound.

"Team leaders check in."

Larry's four team leaders checked in one by one.

Four minutes later, the motorcade pulled up in front of the mansion. On cue, Governor Beachum came out the front door to greet the President and the Vice President.

Four Lincoln SUVs sat there for several minutes. Their glass was tinted black, so it was impossible to see inside. Governor Beachum stood there showing no emotion despite the fact that Champer was clearly trying to humiliate him. Television cameras focused on Beachum, who continued to smile throughout.

Seven minutes after the motorcade had arrived, a Black Hawk grunt stepped out of the SUV in front of the President's and strode to the back door of the President's SUV. He wore a tight short sleeve black shirt and a Kevlar vest. His arms were thick with muscles and covered in tattoos.

He opened the door and out stepped Champer's son and then the President. The President wore a blue summer suit and a red tie.

Beachum strode forward and then the first awkward moment occurred. The Black Hawk operative held his hand out and appeared to put it on Beachum's chest as if holding him away from the President.

Larry, who stood behind and to the left of Beachum tensed. But then the President whispered in the grunt's ear and he moved out of the way.

Governor Beachum and President Champer shook hands. Champer attempted to pull Beachum in — his signature move — but Beachum held his ground. Champer gave him a wickedly evil smile.

Champer's son, Dick Jr., who despite now being the Vice President of the United States, made no effort to shake Beachum's hand. Rather, he had turned to look over the grounds and seemed disinterested in what was happening.

Despite his guest status, Champer extended his arm forward as if to point the way inside.

Less than two-minutes later, they crossed through the ante-room in which many men would be stationed and entered the large conference room where the meeting was to take place. Pool photographers had been set-up to capture stills of the historic meeting, but no media would be allowed in the room for the actual meeting.

After the photos were taken, the media left the room, as did the various aides that had filed in for final preparations.

On one side of the table, facing the window sat the President and the Vice President. On the other side, sat Governor Beachum and his right-hand, Bill Tanner.

Larry stood to the left of the governor with his back to the window. He was unarmed. Two secret service agents stood by the door, while two others stood behind the President. They were all armed.

After some histrionics, Champer and Beachum got down to business.

"Mr. President, I wanted to thank you for coming today, sir."

Champer smiled. "We need to work together, George. To fix this."

Beachum nodded. "We would like that, Mr. President." He paused. "But California cannot stand for some of the things that have been happening."

Champer smiled even more broadly. He then spread out his hands. "What are your demands?

Bill Tanner whispered in Beachum's ear. Beachum then looked down at a piece of paper in front of him. "Our demands as you called them, sir. Our demands would be an immediate suspension of 101-64, a commission consisting of state and federal representatives on the environment, and an agreement from Congress to hold an up and down vote on Witherspoon's comprehensive immigration plan."

Champer continued smiling. "Is that all?"

Beachum and Tanner laughed. "Yes, Mr. President. That's all."

Champer looked at his son and then leaned in and whispered something to him. Dick Jr. nodded his head and then wrote something down. Champer then turned back to Beachum and smiled. "George." He paused. "We will have to work out some of the details especially as it relates to Congress and their buy-in. That said – I have Eric [Senate Majority Leader Douglas] on speed dial and the House and I tend to see eye-to-eye, so I think we can get them over the finish line."

Beachum sat back. Tanner leaned over and whispered to him.

Champer then continued. "Look, George. You won and I lost. But to keep this country great, we need the states to truly be united and that obviously includes California."

After some formalities, the four men rose and took turns shaking hands. Champer again held out his arm as to guide the men out and the Governor and Bill Tanner dutifully led the way out.

As the door opened, Larry immediately knew something was wrong. Although at what could be called a loud whisper, men were arguing. Larry looked through the door and saw three FBI agents arguing with Daxton and Russo. In all, Larry counted eight secret service agents, three Black Hawk grunts, four of his men and the FBI agents in the room. There were no civilians.

With the contingent from the conference room now reentering the ante-room, there were nearly 25 in the room, which was probably five more than capacity.

Larry could feel the world closing in around him as Champer spoke. "Not to be overly dramatic, but arrest these men."

Bill Tanner screamed. "You son-of-a-bitch!"

A Black Hawk grunt, the same one that had opened the President's car door earlier, seemed to push Tanner in the back and he fell forward.

At the same moment, Rusty Russo yelled, "I said, stand down!"

One of the FBI agents drew his weapon. Russo thrust the palm of his right hand into the chin of the agent, knocking him backwards into the wall. The other two agents drew their weapons, as Daxx held up his arms, trying to calm the situation. Larry pushed down the Governor.

"Arrest these men!" Champer yelled again.

A secret service agent who had been in the conference room and now stood to the left of Larry pushed his gun into the small of Larry's back. A moment later, he moved it as all hell broke loose.

One of the Black Hawk grunts pushed Daxton into the wall. Daxton threw back his elbow and the grunt's head snapped back. Secret service guns were now drawn everywhere.

A moment later, someone fired.

As Larry watched the Black Hawk grunt's head snap back, he acted. In retrospect and he had a lot of time over the years to turn it over in his mind, he concluded that he should have simply dropped to his knees and laced his fingers behind his head.

Larry brought down his left hand and disarmed the secret service agent who only moments before had pressed his gun into Larry's back. The man screamed out as Larry had broken his wrist with a quick violent twist.

Larry pivoted and dropped to one knee, pushing the disarmed secret service agent forward into the room where he crashed into several men. Larry picked up the man's Glock as a bullet punched the wall above Larry's head.

Larry got a quick look at the room. Angus Daxton was lying on the floor. He had been shot at close range in the chest. Larry was fairly certain that his

Kevlar vest had stopped the bullet, but at such close range, death was possible.

Men were screaming. Three secret service agents had grabbed the President and pushed him into a running kneel as they ran toward the door through the gauntlet of men.

Larry raised the gun and shot at the three Black Hawk grunts who he gauged to be the biggest threat to the Governor. Two of them fell immediately, but he only winged the third. Larry then pivoted back into the conference room door, which swung into the conference room, as several bullets crashed into the wall – men were firing wildly in the crowded room.

The remaining Black Hawk grunt stood over Daxton and shot him in the back of the head.

Larry brought up his gun again as he continued to backpeddle into the conference room. As he fired at the remaining Black Hawk grunt, his lower back connected with the conference room table thus altering his firing line.

Like a laser guided missile, his bullet cut diagonally across the room toward the exit door and impacted President Richard Champer Sr. just above the left ear. The left side of his head exploded in a mass of bone and tissue. He died instantly.

More bullets were fired as the conference room doors rebounded shut in front of Larry.

Without hesitating, Larry dove shoulder first through the glass window of the conference room. He landed in a shoulder roll and then got to his feet. Most on the property had made a bee-line for the front door when the shooting started. Chaos reigned supreme.

Larry ran diagonally across the front lawn of the compound, expecting to be shot at any second, but everyone appeared focused on the inside of the house. He reached the tree-line and continued running through roughly two-hundred meters of wooded area until he reached the fence line. He hit the fence and in two quick pushes was over the fence.

As he ran, Larry drew his cellphone from his pocket and he opened his contacts. A moment later the phone rang.

"Red Bear!"

"Mother, I'm in trouble."

"Understood. Where are you?"

"I'm on foot, about a kilometer from governor's mansion, heading west."

"Can you get to the Standstead safe house?"

"Yes. Mother, I need you to get Beth and the kids."

"Copy that, Red Bear. We will get them."

"Thanks, mother."

"God speed, Red Bear."

 Larry continued to run.

59

July 2nd, 2034

Los Angeles, California

Dougherty let out a loud hoot. "Holy shit. That is not the way the history books wrote that story."

Kennex interjected. "What's it they say about history being written by the victors?"

Dougherty laughed. "I believe that's what they say – history is written by the victors."

Larry sat back and rubbed his eyes. He had kept that story bottled up for eleven years and it was exhausting to re-tell it, finally, after all these years.

Karen leaned in and she said through what Larry thought were stifled tears, "who killed Beachum and Tanner?"

Larry shook his head. "I don't know. The room was pure chaos and I had pushed the Governor to the ground. Once that door closed, whatever happened after that is unknown to me."

Karen could tell how deeply he regretted what he had just said. He had left the Governor and his men behind. She didn't blame him at all; although a small part of her wanted to. He had just seen his bullet kill the President. Instinct would have driven any man to run in that moment.

"What happened next?"

Larry looked at Karen. He realized he had gone too far to clam up at this point. "I am ex-CIA. My former handler got me to a safe house, which got me out of immediate harm's way. My number one priority was getting my family to safety." As Larry said the last part, his voice trailed off.

Kennex now asked a question. "And you trusted the CIA?"

Larry looked at him for several beats. "No, but I trusted Malcolm Mastriani." He paused. "Besides, I didn't have many options at that point. I had just committed about the highest crime imaginable short of killing Jesus and I had to hope I could trust someone."

"And?" Karen raised her eyebrows as she asked this.

"And Malcolm came through as I knew he would. He mobilized a team to get my family out and activated several assets he had to get me a new identity."

"What happened to your wife? Elizabeth, wasn't it?"

Larry stared at Karen. Tears began to run down his cheeks. "Beth, it was Beth." He wiped his right cheek with the back of his hand. "Malcolm's team was too late. They said she grabbed a gun when the FBI arrived. News reports said she was shot once, but Malcolm later told me that she had been shot six times."

"Those motherfuckers." Ken Dougherty looked down at his feet as he said this.

"And your kids? You had two boys right?"

Larry looked now at Jack Kennex and then shook his head. "I don't know other than before I went dark. Off the grid, Malcolm had gotten them to safety. After I," he paused and framed his face, "had the work done, Malcolm got me a bunch of new identities and I disappeared."

"All due respect, Larry, but how the fuck did you pull that off? The biggest manhunt the world has ever seen is underway and you manage to get your face altered and stay low enough that no one ever tips anyone as to where you might be? I mean, fuck, the reward for you was like a hundred million or something."

Larry stared at Kennex for a while. "The invasion began the day after the incident. California and New York were in state of war, albeit a pretty one-sided one. The world was in a state of chaos. Malcolm was the very best at what he did, including making it pretty clear to anyone that might have tweeted about something that he would disappear them if they did."

Karen interrupted. "Are you still in contact with them?"

Larry nodded although he looked lost in thought. "Not directly with Malcolm. We agreed that once I went dark, we would cut off all communications. But Malcolm hooked me up with a tech who has helped me to avoid anyone's radar these past eleven years."

"He know who you are?" Ken Dougherty had asked the question.

Larry shook his head. "As far as he knows, I am just a guy who has some loose ties to the CIA."

The room got quiet for a while. Cory Nelson went around and filled everyone's water glass as the group contemplated all they had just heard.

Larry finally spoke. "I'm pretty sure the President, the current President, ordered Beachum and Tanner killed in that room that day. His father had just been killed, there was chaos and my gut tells me that's what happened. I am also fairly certain that he or one of his minions ordered my family taken, which at least resulted in Beth's death."

Larry stared off into space for a moment and then turned to Karen and completely changed the subject. "You're Kate Beachum." He said this as a comment and not as a question.

Karen actually gagged on the water she had been drinking and then stared at Larry. "When did you figure that out?"

Larry shook his head. "Just now, but it fits and I guess I had been seeing the resemblance all along and it just didn't register."

Karen brushed her hair with her hand. "I was away at school and then on exchange and I was doing ROTC stuff. I should have come home." She paused in thought. "I should have come home."

Larry now recalled looking at pictures of her throughout the Governor's mansion. She was probably close to twenty years older than she was in most of the pictures, which would have been when she was a pre-teen. He was rusty, but as he stared at her, the resemblance was coming back to him.

"Katie, you'd be in jail now like the rest of your family."

Karen turned to Kennex. "I know that, Jack. But as I have said to you over the years, it doesn't make it any less fucking painful."

Kennex ducked his head. He knew as he said it that it was probably a mistake.

"So what now?" It was the first time that Cory Nelson had asked a question.

Karen looked at Nelson and then at Larry. "If I was 95% before, I am 110% now. We go as planned."

All the men in the room nodded.

60

December 17th, 2023

Washington, District of Columbia

Richard "Dick" Champer Jr. sat at the head of the large conference room table. He had been sworn in on Air Force 1 as the 46th President of the United States the night before. Less than two-weeks earlier, he had been simply the son of the most polarizing President in the history of the United States. Today, he was its President.

The Constitution was silent on the actual status of Dick Jr. He had not yet been confirmed by the Senate and House to be Vice President, but this had not stopped his aides from ordering a swearing in of him as President on the flight back from California.

His father's body was placed in one of the conference rooms aboard the plane. Dick Jr. had spent some time alone with the body. The man who had been the driving force in his life was gone. Dick Jr. thought back to the last words his father had whispered in his ear earlier that day. "I can't wait to see their faces."

The side of his head was gone. Dick Jr. insisted on seeing his father's face – now he regretted it. Those in the room had confirmed that it was

Beachum's head of security, Larry Nash, who pulled the trigger. Dick Jr. had not really taken note of the man during the meeting. The only thing he remembered were his deep blue eyes. Unusually blue. Dick Jr. doubted he would ever forget those eyes. A massive manhunt was immediately launched for Nash and his family.

When Dick Jr. had settled in his father's office on Air Force 1 (now his office), he sat staring out the darkening window for a time. He loved his father deeply and his anger was boiling up inside.

The phone had rung soon after. It was Scott Burnside, who Dick Jr. had spent significant time with over the years. He recognized Burnside as the key strategic planner in his father's career.

While Dick Jr. was familiar with his father and Burnside's plan, Burnside pressed him on the importance of following through. Beachum was dead rather than under arrest and President Champer had died a hero, but in order to guarantee that their efforts to continue to control the levers of power remained intact, California and New York needed to be brought to heel.

Burnside had made it clear to Dick Jr. who his inner circle was - NSA Bob Baker, Secretary of State Jill James and White House Chief Counsel Doug Barret. Everyone else was a leaky wheel and while they were unlikely to cause too many problems, only the inner circle would truly have his back.

It was only his second time in the Situation Room at the White House (the first time had been as part of a tour given by his father), but Dick Jr. now sat at the head of the table surrounded by the Joint Chiefs of Staff, National Security Advisor Bob Baker, the White House Chief of Staff Cal Doggett, and the Secretary of State Jill James.

One wall was full of maps of Europe that showed the current status of the Russian army. Estonia south to Bulgaria and as far west as Poland were now under Russian control. In all, nine formerly independent countries had fallen in a span of six weeks. Current casualty estimates numbered close to thirty-five thousand for the formerly independent countries, while Russian losses were put at under five-thousand.

NATO forces were marked on the map in Germany, Finland, Slovakia and Hungary, but without significant US support, which the late President Champer had been unwilling to provide, NATO stood little chance of turning back the Russians. The Russian advance had abruptly stopped at the end of September. Since then, there had been virtually no dialogue between the NATO allies and Moscow.

Another map showed Asia and the significant activity that was building in China and North Korea. Japan and South Korea had reached out to the US for help, but again, nothing had been forthcoming as of yet.

The various heads of the different military branches had filled in the newly sworn in President on the current global situation report as well as all aspects of Operation United Coast.

The President had had two glasses of scotch before entering the Situation Room. He could feel the alcohol both calming him and giving him a wave of courage. "General, we proceed as planned."

General Wesley Lestifer nodded to the President. "I understand, Mr. President. But I simply wanted to lay out the alternatives in the wake of what took place yesterday."

"What took place yesterday, General, was nothing short of an attempted coup. Beachum and his men tried to overthrow this government and we are going to see that their deeds do not go unpunished." The President squinted his eyes and looked around at the rest of the people at the table as he said this.

Bob Baker, who had been one of his father's biggest and earliest supporters, nodded his head at the President. "I agree, sir. We have already essentially put the first phase of United Coast into effect, despite yesterday's tragic events. From a legal perspective, you have the right and the duty to act."

Lestifer interrupted. "All due respect to Mr. Baker, but we have the situation in Europe, which threatens to deteriorate further, as well as a significant movement of Chinese assets to the south and east. I fear that if we become too focused on Operation UC, we may end up taking our eye off the ball as it relates to the rest of the world."

Baker leaned over and whispered something in the President's ear.

Several of the military brass looked at one another and then at Cal Doggett. No one looked particularly comfortable with where things were headed and Doggett appeared to be viewed as the last hope for de-escalation.

Doggett cleared his throat. He doubted that he could talk down the hardliners in Champer's Administration. However, history was fraught with men who had ignored their principles and this felt like just such a moment to him. He looked back at that various faces that had centered on him. He remained silent.

"General Lestifer?" President Champer rose to his feet, his hands pressed against the table, and then looked at the General and around the room before once again locking eyes with Lestifer. He waited for him to answer.

"Yes, Mr. President?"

Champer paused for effect. "You are a go for phase 2 of Operation United Coast."

61

February 14th, 2025

New York, New York

Lester Hollis cut down Lexington Avenue and then turned left on 88th street. He knew there was a checkpoint at 86th and 3rd Avenue and he needed to avoid it.

He crossed over 3rd at 88th and kept walking down to 2nd Avenue. He was far enough from the checkpoint that no one gave him any problems, despite the color of his skin.

Lester was black, which didn't tend to arouse too much suspicion, but he was fairly light-skinned and had spent most of his life being mistaken for Latino. Over the past year-and-a-half, since martial law (or Champer Law as the locals had come to call it) had been declared in New York City and sections of New York State, Lester had had a series of run-ins with the military and the federal police that most had started calling "the gestapo."

He carried his citizen card at all times and his name did not have a Latino sound to it, but the gestapo still got its rocks off rousting the innocent.

However, Lester would usually tolerate the checkpoints to get to where he needed to get to, but today he had misplaced his phone. He was sure he had left it on the end table next to his bed, but he had tied one on the night before with the little vodka he had left and the night had been a bit of a haze. This morning, the phone was nowhere to be found and Lester had to get to work.

As he walked down 88th, he passed underneath a large billboard that declared Champer's Second Rule: Cell Phones Must Be Carried At All Times.

Lester, who had gone to Queens College and had studied to become a paralegal while there, was fairly certain that all of Champer's Rules were unconstitutional. But the Supreme Court had yet to do anything about it and with New York and as far as he knew California still under Champer's Law, Lester didn't imagine a court of law would give a shit.

Lester rounded on to 2nd Avenue and nearly collided with a group of six federal police. "Where you going, ese?"

Lester stopped and looked at the 30-something dark haired cop. "Just going to work, officer." Lester smiled and made sure he spoke in perfect English.

The cop frowned. "Which bodega you work at, ese?"

Lester smiled. "I work at a law firm, officer."

The cop stared at him. "You a lawyer, ese?"

Lester shook his head. "No sir, a paralegal. I help the lawyers at the firm with their cases."

"What's your name?" Another cop, this one about ten years older and needing to lose 50-pounds, asked the question.

"Lester Hollis, sir."

"You got ID, Lester?" A third cop, this one blond-haired, clean-cut and roughly the same age as the first cop.

Lester fished in his front pocket and handed over his citizen card. The cop who had asked for it, slowly paged through it.

"Lester a fake name? You really Lupe or something like that?" The blond cop asked Lester. The other cops all laughed.

Lester continued smiling. "No sir, it's Lester."

"Let me scan your phone, Lester. I want to see where you been today." It was the first cop asking.

Lester continued smiling. "I'm sorry, officer, but I could not find it this morning and I had to get to work."

The cop made a tsk tsk sound. "Lester, you know that's against the rules. We could arrest you for that. Hell, we could practically shoot you for that."

"I know, officer. I looked for it and I must have dropped it behind the couch or something and ..."

"Shut the fuck up, Lester." It was the clean-cut cop.

Lester put his head down. "Yes, sir."

"Maybe we should just put a bullet in poor Lester and save the hassle?" It was a fourth cop, who said this eliciting more laughter.

The cops made Lester stand with his face against the wall. They ordered him to look straight ahead. One of them, he couldn't see which, phoned in and asked about warrants on a Lester Jeremy Hollis. Lester was unable to hear what came back, but he assumed they found nothing. Ten and then twenty minutes went by and Lester continued to stare straight ahead.

Lester felt someone walk past. The footsteps stopped and a woman's voice said, "Excuse me, young man, but is everything all right?"

Lester reluctantly turned his head to see an older white woman carrying a grocery bag. He then turned all the way around.

The cops were gone. Lester would be late for work.

62

December 17th, 2023

Elk Grove, California

"Confirm, we have four inside."

"You are a go."

The eleven Black Hawk operatives came up at the house from four sides. They were armed with M249 light machine guns.

Three men reached the front door. One held a battering ram. After two beats, he hit the door with the ram as another said into his mic, "go, go, go."

Along one side of the house, two men tossed concussion grenades through the living room window. Two others came crashing through the back door.

Shots were fired.

Although inaudible from the outside, a dying woman whispered, "Cody, daddy will come for you."

63

December 17ᵗʰ, 2023

Elk Grove, California

"Confirm, we have one deceased, a woman. One wounded, also a woman. We are in route to the rendezvous point with two children."

"Copy, well done, red team."

Jamie Wells sat back and looked out the passenger window of the Lincoln Navigator SUV. He could see the second SUV in front of theirs, while he knew there was a third right behind.

The two kids in the back seat had stopped crying and the smaller one, who Wells figured was five or six, had fallen asleep. The older one continued to tell Jamie and the three other men in the SUV that his father was going to get them.

"Hey kid, do us a favor and give it a rest." It was the driver Dennis "the Menace" O'Neil.

"He's going to get you first."

The four men laughed. Wells had to admit that the kid had spunk. He had just seen his mother killed and he was immediately looking for vengeance.

"Maybe so, sport. But not today, so can we slow it down, at least for now?"

The boy folded his arms and seemed to quiet down. He again began to cry. Wells had to admit that he felt bad for the kid, but considering what his dad had done, his life was unlikely to get better from here.

They approached a traffic light that had just gone green. Wells continued to scan the surroundings. He was most worried about running into cops; although, the White House had guaranteed him that they would not be harassed by the locals on this mission.

The light changed from green to yellow to red. Wells stared at the light, momentarily confused. Man, that was a quick light, he thought almost subconsciously to himself.

The truck in front slowed to a stop. Wells looked around. There was nothing of note.

A moment later, the right side of the SUV in front of theirs exploded. The SUV toppled over to the left. A second explosion followed behind them.

Wells yelled, "get us the fuck out of here!"

O'Neil turned the wheel to the left and stomped the gas. His head then exploded. The truck bucked to a stop

Wells twisted to the right and ducked down, he could hear two more bullet impacts. He unbuckled his seatbelt and opened his door, rolling out.

He felt a punch to his stomach. His vest had stopped the bullet, but he was badly winded.

Wells raised his M249 and fired wildly. A second bullet hit him in the left shoulder and then continued through the back of his neck, spinning Wells around as the gun flew from his hands. Wells hit the ground face down.

As he lay there, Wells thought to himself, "the fuckin' kid was right." Moments later, Wells began to choke on his own blood. 45-seconds later, he was dead.

64

December 25ᵗʰ, 2023

East Los Angeles, California

Manuel "Manny" Rodriguez stared at his wife and two children. They were camped out in the back room of the small East LA bodega he and his now deceased father had spent the past 15-years getting off the ground.

Through the walls, they could hear the sirens and occasional volleys of gunfire. From time to time, they also heard screaming, but after two days of constant engagement, the screams were fewer and farther between.

Manny had ventured out the night before to the front of the store to get a look through the metal slats in the security gate that protected the window. A fire raged across the street at what had been a discount electronics store and there appeared to be a dead body lying at the corner of Turner and Van Buren, which was about 200 meters from the bodega's window. Manny didn't see any soldiers or any other signs of life.

Power was out, so Manny had taken a case of warm bottled water from the shelves and two boxes of saltines and some Cocoa Puffs with him to the back room.

His wife and kids were still sleeping. Manny listened to the radio, which was tuned to the only news station he could find that had not gone quiet over the past two-days.

"We repeat as we have been instructed to do, all citizens of California are ordered to stay in your homes. Any unauthorized individuals caught outside will be subject to arrest."

Manny had been just opening the store when he heard the rumble of what turned out to be a group of army troop carriers heading down Van Buren Boulevard.

Manny ran upstairs to their small apartment above the store and ordered his wife Janine to take the kids downstairs to the bodega. They had all watched from the window as the soldiers had moved in. Several troop carriers, jeeps and one city bus made their way down the street with a group of about 100 soldiers, machine guns drawn, in front of them.

Loudspeakers blared from the troop carriers that rolled in. "All citizens, please assemble on the street for inspection."

Manny had told Janine to take the kids to the back room. He watched as some people dutifully assembled outside of the shops and apartments. Army soldiers approached them and one by one appeared to check identification. Most were told to to assemble in Chessen Park, which was a small park just up the street. However, others were immediately taken into custody and placed on the bus.

For about an hour, things appeared to be fairly orderly and then shots rang out.

Manny could not see from his vantage point where the shots came from, but a soldier almost directly in front of his store was hit. Manny couldn't tell for fear of being seen, but he thought the man was hit in the leg.

Rather than trying to locate where the shots had come from, soldiers opened up on the building across the street from Manny's. He watched as the soldiers almost quite literally obliterated the building in a hail of gunfire.

More shots rang out, this time from Manny's side of the street and Manny saw at least two more soldiers drop. The soldiers took cover behind parked cars and again appeared to blindly return fire.

And then the people in Chessen Park had decided to run. Manny could only see the front side of the park, but people seemed to scatter in all directions. The soldiers in the street began firing and Manny watched as several men, women and children dropped like flies.

Manny had retreated to the back with his family. Six hours later, the power went out as did the internet connection on Manny's phone.

Manny continued to stare at his sleeping kids and then slowly began to move the radio dial. The news station was providing mostly warnings, but no real news.

Manny moved up and down the dial and then caught a static-filled connection. He tuned the dial back and forth until he managed to get a mostly clean signal.

"And those reports continue to be quite grim, folks. We are hearing that thousands are dead in the areas of Boyle Heights, Walnut Park, Bell Gardens and East Los Angeles. The US military appears to have targeted heavily populated Latino areas and they have been rounding up people. Anyone who resists has been engaged."

"Tommy, this is America, how is this happening?" A woman asked the man who had just commented.

"I know, Linda, I know. The invasion and that's what it is, folks, an invasion, that began yesterday in California and New York appears to be this government's reaction to the California vote and the assassination of the President."

The woman named Linda responded. "If you are listening to this broadcast, please stay inside and be safe. If you happen to be an illegal, stay underground as all reports we have been getting are that you will be arrested or worse."

Manny stared at Janine who was now awake and staring at him. She wiped a tear from her left cheek.

Janine then spoke in a whisper. "My father used to talk about America until late into the night. He'd tell us how one day, he would take us there and we'd be free and..." her voice trailed off. She was silent for a couple of minutes.

"Did you know he gave me an American name because he was certain he would bring us here one day?"

Manny shook his head. She had told him this before, but he did not have the heart to tell her at that moment.

"And then he did. And even when my mother didn't make it out, he said it was too important to stop and he got my brother and I here..." her voice again trailed off. Tears now ran down both of Manny's cheeks. He was too heartbroken to speak.

"I thought the family separations were the worst thing I would ever see in my lifetime. My father cried himself to sleep when he saw that. This wasn't the America he told us about."

Manny nodded.

"He wasn't an educated man, Manny. But, my God, he was smarter than any of those pendejos in Washington." She paused and gulped some water. "He would talk about how we, meaning America, had lost all of its empathy. These are human beings, the same as whether they were born in Santa Monica or San Salvador."

Manny wiped the tears from his cheeks, he was unable to speak. He realized for the first time that it was Christmas.

"When did we lose empathy, Manny?"

Manny took a deep breath in. He could not look at her for a moment for fear of breaking down. He heard a voice yell from the street; although, through the walls, all he could make out was "ASAP."

65

December 25th, 2023

East Los Angeles, California

"Disengage immediately!"

All around him soldiers continued to open fire on the crowd as it ran every which way from the park about one hundred meters in front of their position.

Kennex grabbed the soldier that stood in front of him by the shoulder and yanked him backwards. "I said disengage!"

The solider stared blankly back at Kennex; however, several others continued to fire. Kennex watched as what looked to be a kid no older than five or six go down.

Kennex's phone chirped. "This is Captain Kennex, over."

"Kennex, what the hell is going on down there?" The voice of Colonel Ryan Manning barked through the phone.

Kennex looked around. The shooting had momentarily stopped. The building to his left had been almost completely obliterated by the onslaught that had taken place only moments before, while the crowd that his men had assembled in the park was either lying dead or wounded in the street or had fled the area.

"Sir, we have multiple locals down in the street." Kennex's voice betrayed his revulsion at the events that had just unfolded.

"Captain, were you engaged?"

"Yes, sir, we took some random fire, but …"

Manning cut him off. "Captain, continue to clean it up. I want you to go door to door if you have to."

Kennex paused and again looked at the massacre that had just unfolded around him. "Sir, we have unarmed civilians down in the street, including women and children. Request multiple medics for immediate evac, over."

Manning did not immediately respond. Another voice then cut in. "Kennex, clean up the area and then we will worry about the wounded."

Kennex recognized the voice of Lieutenant Joe Baker. The two had once served together in Afghanistan and then later in the army reserves. He hated Baker with a passion largely because Baker was a card-carrying racist, who reveled in hurting anyone who was not white.

"Sir, we have children down in the street. In my view …"

"Captain, I did not ask for your fucking view. You have your orders, now clean it up or I will get someone else to clean it up."

The line went dead. Kennex looked at his men who were squatting in various positions amongst the parked cars, guns trained on the buildings that lined both sides of the street. In the distance, a woman had begun to call out for help. She appeared to be amongst the wounded in the street.

Kennex's mouth was dry. His men had begun to look over the shoulders at him, awaiting their orders. He had no doubt that if they started to go door to door, more civilians were going to die.

Kennex looked across at a man squatting about ten feet to his right. "Sergeant Zillow."

Zillow, who was about a foot shorter than Kennex, scrambled over, keeping his head low. Kennex continued to stand straight and tall, so the difference in their heights was accentuated.

"Yes, Captain?"

Kennex stared at Zillow. He had only known him for about a month, but Kennex had become instantly fond of Zach "Sleepy" Zillow. While small in stature, Zillow was tough and smart and had a booming voice that men instantly wanted to follow, despite the size of the man delivering the message.

"Sergeant, I am about to violate a direct order."

Zillow stared up at Kennex. He now rose to his full height, which narrowed the gap by about a foot, but still left Zillow's neck craning sharply up. Zillow then looked around and then back at Kennex. "Understood, sir."

"Sergeant, I have been ordered to go door to door and clean up the locals. I want you to help those people." Kennex pointed at those who had fallen outside of the park. "I then want you to place me under arrest."

Zillow stared at Kennex for two beats and then nodded. He then keyed his radio, which was attached to his left breast. "This is Sergeant Zillow. We have been ordered to tend to the wounded."

The men turned in unison to stare back at Kennex and Zillow. Zillow then boomed, "I want those wounded tended to ASAP!"

The men snapped to and began moving down the street. Zillow turned back to Kennex. He stared at him for several seconds and then slammed the butt of his machine gun down into Kennex's knee. Kennex crumbled to the ground, writhing in pain.

"Peterson, we need a medic for the captain. He appears to have been wounded in the fray."

66

January 11ᵗʰ, 2024

Washington, District of Columbia

"My fellow Americans, it had been nearly four-weeks since the murder ..." President Champer stopped and looked to his right at Scott Burnside. "I don't like leading with the murder. And I think we should call it an assassination."

Burnside nodded. He turned to Bob Baker, who sat on the couch of the Oval Office, the television camera just in front of him. "Thoughts?"

"I agree with POTUS. I think we go with the original set-up for the speech, which had us leading with the situations in California and New York. America..." he paused. "Free America needs to know that the situation is now under control and that we will maintain a state of martial law on the coasts for the time being."

"Jill?" Burnside looked at Secretary of State Jill James, who stood in the camera position. "I concur. I also think we need to inform people of how the manhunt is going for Nash."

Champer looked at Chris Coolidge, who he had just named as acting head of the FBI on the instruction of Burnside. Coolidge was a bit of a right wing crazy, but he was loyal and had an extensive law enforcement background, having been a sheriff in Texas for 25-years. Coolidge stood off to the side of the room, near the Chief of Staff's door.

"We have barely had a sniff since the initial tip on the safe-house he went to just after the incident. We are fairly certain he is still in California as the military has it locked down tight and with martial law in effect, his ability to move around is limited, but I will level with you, Mr. President, we have few leads at present."

Champer sighed. "What do we know about this guy?"

Baker interjected. "He's ex-Army Ranger, ex-CIA and about as tough as they come. There was nothing in his MO that would suggest he would ever go rogue like this. Further..." he paused to scratch his chin, "he is probably well connected to some pretty tough hombres, who are loyal to a fault."

"And his kids?" Burnside had effectively ordered the President to grab Nash's kids to use as leverage to draw him out. He had also thought that the death of Nash's wife would be convenient as the press did not need to hear what a patriot this guy had been. He had made sure that in the wake of her death, the press had been given a story about how she used one of her kids as a human shield in the fire fight that had taken place.

Coolidge responded. "As Mr. Baker noted, Nash was well connected to some pretty tough hombres. They took out the Black Hawk team in a matter of seconds. Eleven dead, including Jamie Wells, who I once went hunting with and was one of the toughest son-of-a-gun's you'd ever want to meet."

Champer weighed in. "So his kids are just gone too?"

Coolidge nodded. "Our thesis is that they are not in California. Nash was either paranoid or really smart because we do not have many images of his kids that appear to be at all recent. The Black Hawks filmed the scene that day, but all of their phones and equipment are gone and probably destroyed. These guys are about as professional as they come, so I think it's a safe bet that we don't find the kids unless someone talks or makes a big stinkin' mistake and I put low odds on that."

Champer snapped back. "So let me get this straight. We think this Nash guy probably accidentally killed my father, so he had no plan to do this. And then he escapes in the melee and somehow, mobilizes over 48-hours the escape not only of himself, but of his kids and nearly of his whole family?"

While Coolidge had many flaws, bullshit was not one of them. "That's correct, sir. Our thesis remains that the attempted arrest of the late Governor Beachum touched off a series of events that culminated in the death of the President. We have no evidence that there was any pre-planning on the part of Nash and the witness testimony from those in the room suggest that Nash was trying to save his men with one swearing that he was sighting someone else with the fatal shot."

"I was in the fucking room, Chris!"

Coolidge nodded. "Yes, sir. Of course, sir."

The room was quiet for about thirty-seconds.

Burnside now spoke. "Okay, I think we hit them with the current status of the invasion then roll into the current status of Europe..." he looked at the President. "We have that called scheduled later with President Popov."

The President nodded and Burnside continued. "We then follow that with the status of the Nash investigation and conclude with the VP pick to leave a good taste in their mouths." Burnside looked around the room. "That good with everyone." They all nodded.

"Okay, Mr. President. Let's dry run it once and then we go live." Burnside gave President Champer a thumbs up as he said this.

The President nodded. He cleared his throat and then looked at the camera. "My fellow Americans..."

67

January 12, 2024

Santa Barbara, California

Larry sat on the couch watching the television news. The only news broadcasting in California was Fox. He was unsure if this was the case outside of California. They were running snippets of the President's speech the night before, calling it alternatively "inspired", "courageous", and something that would have "made his father proud."

Larry held an ice pack to his right cheek. It continued to throb more than a week later. He had a hand mirror by his side that he checked periodically. The bandages had only been off for a day and the swelling was significant. That said – Larry was admittedly a bit shocked by his new face.

Larry's arm also hurt. The doctor had decided to remove the scar on Larry's left arm from a bullet that had hit him a decade before. The scar would have been easy to trace if he were ever caught for something, so better safe than sorry.

Lastly, Larry's fingers were numb from heavy pain killers that he had to inject every four hours. The final piece of the puzzle was grafted finger prints, a procedure Larry was thankful he would never have to endure again.

Larry's phone buzzed. It was a burner he had been given the day before by the hosts of the small basement apartment in which he currently dwelled. He was not exactly sure where he was as the past few days had been a haze and his handlers thought it best that he not know where he was going, but he could hear the ocean close by, so he assumed they were near the beach.

Larry struggled to click the phone as his fingers were still useless. Finally, he pressed it with his nose. A voice spoke immediately. "This is the last time you will hear from me." Larry instantly recognized Malcolm's voice.

"I understand." Larry paused. "I, ummm, have no way to thank you for this."

Malcolm laughed. "I could count on both hands and feet the number of thanks I owe you for saving my fat ass over the years."

"If you say so." Larry's voice trailed off.

Malcolm switched to all business, a tone Larry had grown familiar with over the years. "Everything is all set. The packages are safe and secure. If you reach under the couch, you will see a package of your own. That has everything you need."

Larry nodded even though he was on the phone. "Copy that, mother."

"Good luck, Red Bear." Larry wasn't sure, but he thought Malcolm's voice cracked as he said it. Malcolm then clicked off.

Larry put down the phone and reached under the couch. He located a small manila envelope. In it, he found four identities – Larry Stabler, which had a post-it attached to it that said "primary", John Lawrence, Dan LaRusso, and Carl Weathers. Despite the pain in his face and arm and the numbness in his hands, Larry began laughing uncontrollably.

He then dozed off from the pain and the medication. His last thoughts were of his wife and of the All Valley Karate Championship.

68

July 3rd, 2034

Los Angeles, California

Karen wiped the cobwebs from her eyes. She had spent the day planning with Cory Nelson and waiting anxiously for Larry and Jack to come home from work. While the port should technically be closed today, because of the arrival of the President, all workers had been ordered in to go over the schedule for his arrival the next day.

When Larry and Jack had walked in, she had to resist the urge to embrace Larry. She had known him for less than two weeks and yet, she was falling for a man who was almost old enough to be her father. Or at least her much older brother, she thought to herself.

Larry and Jack reported nothing unusual at the docks that day. They had made sure to do their daily routines to a tee and then had made their way back to 14 Wesson.

Karen, Larry, Kennex, Ken Dougherty, Nelson and Phil Richards gathered in the living room around a plate of sandwiches to go over the plan for tomorrow.

"These eat a lot better than they wear," noted Ken Dougherty, holding up one of the sandwiches to Larry in a nod to the other night.

They all shared a laugh and then Karen spoke. "Larry, I have some good news and bad news - we will have another asset on the ground at the docks."

Larry raised his eyebrows in surprise. "What's the bad news?"

Karen gave a half smile. "We will have another asset on the ground at the docks."

Larry looked around the room. "I don't follow."

Karen nodded. "There is a woman who is sympathetic to FOB, who we now have intel will be there tomorrow. She is a part of the President's security detail."

Larry looked at Kennex. "How reliable is this?"

Kennex took a bite of a turkey sandwich and shrugged. "We've never worked with her on an operation for obvious reasons, but she has provided valuable information over the years when we have needed it."

Larry looked at Karen. "She was the one who provided the intel on the President being at the docks." He said this as a statement more than a question.

Karen nodded. "She was originally only going to be on the advance team, but she got word to us today that she would be on the protection team tomorrow."

Larry sat lost in thought for a moment and then replied. "What's she prepared to do?"

Karen looked at Phil Richards. "Phil's been her handler over the years."

Richards put down his sandwich and wiped his mouth with a napkin. "I'm not sure. I think she is a believer in our vision of America, but she has a family – a husband, two kids. She's been content to exist on the periphery and that's been fine with us. This will be the first time she will be in the line of fire so to speak as it relates to an operation."

"She's going to be in danger tomorrow." Larry replied.

Karen nodded. "Hence the good news and bad news."

Larry looked around the room at the various faces. "I'm not sure I love this. We are going to be threading a needle here and we are going to have one of our own assets out there who we may end up taking out in the crossfire. We also don't know whether she potentially burns us because people do funny things when their lives are in danger."

"What do you want to do, Larry?" Richards asked the question.

Larry contemplated for about 30-seconds. "I think we still go, but you all need to be comfortable with potentially losing our own people tomorrow."

"And if she burns us?" Jack Kennex looked at Larry.

Larry took a bite of his sandwich. He had no answer for Kennex, so he simply shrugged.

69

March 18, 2024

Nanliao, Taiwan

Chih-ming Wu walked down the narrow dock to his small outrigger trawler. The sun had started to rise and Wu knew that he would have to get the boat readied quickly for the days catch.

The air was warm, which caught Wu by surprise. March was usually a bit on the chilly side and the weather had been rough for the past couple of weeks.

Wu reached his boat and quickly got to work organizing his gear. He unfolded his nets carefully and ran through a quick check of the ship as the last thing he wanted was to discover a problem while out in the Taiwan Strait.

Satisfied that he was ready to embark, Wu fired up the engines and untied the mast lines from their dock moorings. He then deftly maneuvered the boat through the narrow lanes and prepared to hit the open waters, gradually opening her up.

Wu looked out at the horizon to the north. Although the water was fairly calm where he was, Wu swore that the distant horizon was portraying a far different sea.

Wu slowed the engine and climbed to the bow of the ship where he stood. He cursed himself silently for not having the binoculars his wife had given him for his last birthday. Instead, he cupped his hands around his eyes and squinted against the rising light.

Wu still couldn't make it out, but if he had to guess, a wave of some size was heading toward Nanliao. He thought about his wife and kids briefly, and a feeling of panic moved to his belly.

Wu looked around. The day was perfectly calm and yet he was certain that a giant wave was about to strike the island. Something didn't fit.

He cupped his hands again and squinted. The wave was much closer and now he realized that there were small spaces in the wave. He then heard the planes.

Wu looked up as six Chengdu J-20 stealth fighters streaked over the Taiwanese coast. His small boat continued to amble forward.

Wu looked back at the wave and now realized it was not a wall of water, but a wall of ships approaching. Wu looked up and down the horizon, there had to be hundreds of ships he thought to himself.

Wu scrambled back to mid-ship and powered up the engine. He turned the small trawler, but in the short time it had taken him to get back to the helm, the Chinese warships had cut the distance to about 500 meters. They were closing fast.

He managed to get the ship turned and then went to full throttle. The Chinese fleet continued to close.

Wu reached the edges of small port and he slowed the engine – too many things he could collide with to remain at full power.

He heard the cruiser before he saw it. He turned to starboard and looked up at a small Chinese cruiser that was running ahead of the larger fleet. Wu reflexively raised his arm in greeting to four Chinese sailors that stared down at him from the deck of their ship. They did not wave back.

One of the sailors called out something that Wu could not make out. A moment later, the three others raised machine guns and fired.

Wu died instantly. In all, the three men fired 140 rounds into Wu's boat. It sank in 45-seconds.

Chih-ming Wu would be the first casualty of the war.

70

August 19th, 2024

Washington, District of Columbia

Mitch Peters squinted and looked at President Champer. "Mr. President, you have a record of those who voted for Hillary Clinton in 2016 and for Tynan in 2020, are you saying that the US government will not use that information against people in the 2024 election?"

Champer looked flabbergasted. "Mitch, you know as well as I do that the accusations that have been coming from the left are ridiculous. We would never use how people voted against them as that would be against the very fabric of what makes America great and would fly in the face of what my father believed before he was ruthlessly gunned down by a domestic terrorist."

Peters leaned in. "But what about reports that part of the security measures in California and New York revolves around how people voted in prior elections?"

Champer smiled. "Mitch, we need to keep this country safe. We, no I, will use all tools at my disposal to keep this country safe. Does this mean that we are screening those who look to leave New York and California on a variety of different metrics? Absolutely, Mitch, absolutely. I will not have innocent people hurt because we did not use everything at our disposal to make sure that the undesirables stay behind the barbed wire fences, so to speak."

"But ..."

"But, Mitch, this does not mean that people should not feel free to vote in November for who they think is the best candidate. The notion that this government would use it against them in some way if they did not vote for me is ridiculous. Frankly, Mitch, it is another sign that the Democrats are desperate."

Peters smiled and looked at the camera. "That's good enough for us, Mr. President. You are watching Fox News. This is Peters on Politics with our very special guest, President Richard Champer Jr. We'll be back with our last segment after this."

The two sat issuing mostly small talk during the commercial break. Peters had warned the President before the interview that their mics would be hot throughout the interview and it was better to not chitchat too much when off camera.

"We're back with the 46th President of the United States, Richard Champer Jr. Mr. President, I would be remiss if I did not ask about the pursuit of Larry Nash."

Champer squinted at Peters and fought the urge to look to his right at the image of Nash, which had been put up on the screen behind them. He had studied the image of Nash for months and his deep blue eyes were now burned in Champer's psyche. "The FBI is hard at work turning over all leads in the investigation. Meanwhile, the reward is now up to $250 million for any information that leads to Nash's arrest. We'll get him, Mitch, it's just a matter of time."

Peters could tell that this was not an issue to press with Champer as it tended to show weakness. "Any last things you'd like to say to the American people, Mr. President?"

Champer turned to the camera. "We are doing great. The situations in New York and California are under control and we will be holding a free and fair election this November. The fake news likes to harp on a lot of stuff that is simply not true, but I think people are smart enough to realize what the truth is."

Peters smiled. "Thanks, Mr. President."

Champer nodded. "Thank you, Mitch."

71

October 18th, 2031

Birmingham, Alabama

Scott Rumphy stared out the tiny window. The sky was darkening and the last fingers of sunlight were disappearing over the horizon. He found this part of the day the toughest – bad memories and little hope.

Rumphy turned away from the window and sat down on his bed.

"You solve the problems of the world, sport?"

Rumphy looked at his roommate with a slight smile on his face. "Not today, maybe tomorrow."

Rick Newsome went back to writing on a legal pad. After a few moments of silence, Rumphy spoke again. "You writing another appeal?"

Newsome didn't look up, but gave a slight laugh. "Fuck you."

Two of Governor George Beachum's former aides had been friends for twenty years and now roommates at the Birmingham Supermax for the past two years.

Rumphy started laughing as well. "Seriously, what are you writing?"

Newsome looked up. "I don't really know. Maybe my manifesto. What the hell else am I going to do with 23-hours a day?"

Rumphy turned away and stared through the bars at the cell directly across from them. He could see Oscar Dicks taking a crap and quickly turned away to give the man at least a sliver of privacy.

"So what do you have so far?"

Newsome stared at Rumphy. "I was thinking about England."

"What about England?"

Newsome made a face. "I think about England a lot. Hundreds of years ago they were a kingdom and the monarchy had basically absolute authority. But gradually Parliament whittled this power away. At some point, they became co-equal branches of power in Britain, but then Parliament gradually took more and more power from the monarchy until eventually the king had no power at all."

Rumphy shook his head. "What does that have to do with anything?"

Newsome gave a slight smile. "It doesn't really. But I think about it a lot because I feel like we went in exactly the opposite direction. We had Founding Fathers that put together a pretty amazing document. And this document essentially gave parliament unfettered power. We like to think that the Constitution talks about three co-equal branches of government, but in reality, it doesn't – Congress is granted most of the power."

"How so?" Rumphy enjoyed the frequent philosophical discussions he and Newsome had engaged in over the past two years since they had been reunited at the Alabama prison – it was one of the only ways to pass the endless days.

"If you actually look at the document, really go through it, Congress has the authority to make laws, get rid of laws, override the Executive and ultimately get rid of the Executive and the Judicial if it is not satisfied with the way they are conducting their affairs. It's not easy for them to do these things. Fuck, it's not supposed to be easy. But they were given this power, which makes Congress the all-powerful branch and not co-equal with the other two."

"But?"

"Yeah, "but". Unlike England, our parliament decided over 250-years and especially the last 50 to allow this power to get whittled away. Eventually, the Executive could essentially do what it wanted through executive orders and undeclared wars and by appointing judges that would continually lengthen the rope given to the

Executive. We went from co-equal branches that were really dominated by parliament to co-equal branches that became completely dominated by the monarch."

"And now?"

Newsome shook his head. "There is no now anymore. The Constitution is now just a piece of paper. Our presence in this super max hellhole is testament to that as is all the other shit that is going on in the world."

A buzzer sounded overhead. It was ten minutes to lights out.

The two men were quiet for a minutes and then Rumphy spoke. "How do you think this ends?"

Newsome stared at him for a few beats. "I hope eventually someone gives the Champers their comeuppance."

"And what comes after that?"

Newsome shrugged. "I hate to admit that I have no fucking clue. I'd like to hope that the great piece of paper that our Founding Fathers put together 250-years ago starts to get read again and understood and followed, but considering that those in power would essentially be cutting themselves off at the knees by doing this, I'm pretty sure it's false hope."

The lights went out.

A moment later, they heard footsteps coming down the corridor.

"You guys up?"

"Hey, Jimmy. Newsome was just walking me through why the English are better than we are."

James "Jimmy" Bienemy stared through the bars at the two dark shapes. He had befriended Newsome and Rumphy almost immediately when they had come to the newly built prison two years before. Even though they had been tagged as "enemy combatants" and as a guard at the prison, he should keep his distance, Jimmy liked to listen to them talk, He frequently visited after lights out.

Rumphy whispered. "What's happening out there, Jimmy?"

"Mostly the same. They have finished the Mexico wall and are talking about shutting down the Canadian border. They also once and for all pulled the plug on CNN. Not sure, but I think they threw most of them in jail."

Newsome laughed. "Surprised it took so fucking long."

Bienemy shifted his feet. "Fox is talking all about the 22nd Amendment and how the President and Congress should do away with it."

Newsome sighed. "Guess it was just a matter of time for that one."

Rumphy weighed in. "So that's it then? Champer serves for life? Don't they need like most of Congress and the states to support that?"

Bienemy leaned into the bars. "Fox is saying that with New York and California officially restricted and with five other states on watch, the majorities might be there to get it done."

There was silence for about a minute and then Rumphy spoke. "What's the mood out there, Jimmy?"

"Tough to say. Most people watch Fox 24/7, so they are getting fed a certain story all the time. Their lives are pretty good and while some don't love what this country has become, if there's food on the table and jobs to he had, who cares about the Constitution."

Newsome laughed again. "I suppose the poor bastards in New York and California care. And I think Rumples and I care. Don't we, Rumples?"

"Easy there, Rick. Jimmy is just trying to help."

Bienemy lowered his head and looked at his shoes in the darkness. "I'm sorry, Rick. There are people out there who care a lot about what's happening and not just those in California and New York. I think the problem is that no one has a clue what to do about it."

Newsome turned on his side away from the bars. "When someone figures it out, let us know, would ya?"

Bienemy thought about answering and then walked away.

72

June 7th, 2034

Santa Monica, California

Corporal Roy English drove steadily down the PCH. The sun was beginning to set and he had to fight the urge to look out over the Pacific. With General Pat Parsons riding shotgun in the jeep, he did not want to appear distracted at all. English continually checked his rearview mirror to make sure the troop carrier that was supposed to be following them had not fallen too far behind.

Parsons had taken over as CTO (California Theater of Operation) Commander in early 2034. He had cut his teeth leading US forces in helping the Russians clean up Finnish insurgencies, a mission that suffered almost no US casualties, and his "reward" had been as "overseer" of sorts of the California mission.

Parsons predecessor, General Darryl Kellerman, had been seen by many in the Champer Administration as too soft on the various insurgencies that popped up in California. He had been especially reluctant to go aggressively after the so called FOB movement, which had bloodied the nose of the occupational forces repeatedly over the past five-years.

English noted that they were passing the site of what used to be Pepperdine University. English's older brother used to tell him stories about Pepperdine, which was situated on the cliffs overlooking the Pacific Ocean. According to his brother, the students would go to class in bathing suits and bikinis, which had always seemed to Roy like the coolest thing in all the world.

As they drove past, English noted the large fuel trucks that turned in to what was now a staging area for the US Navy.

For another ten-minutes or so, the two drove in silence. English was very uncomfortable sitting so close to Parsons. He had a reputation for chewing up and spitting out his subordinates, so English was laser-focused on making sure the ride was smooth and Parsons had no reason to get upset.

Other than the occasional fuel truck, the PCH was bereft of traffic as the skies began to darken. A sign warned that the Pacific Palisades were to the left and again English was reminded of some story his brother had once told him, but he could not put his finger on what it was. He checked his rearview mirror, the truck was about 50-feet behind.

As they hit a straightaway, English gave a bit more to the accelerator. At the same moment, gunfire began pelting the jeep from the hillside above. At first English was unsure of what was happening and then Parsons calmly said, "Corporal, we are taking fire."

English yanked the wheel hard to the right, sending the jeep into a slight spin that English quickly pulled it out from. They stopped in what was an old beach parking lot. Gunfire continued to sear the side of the open-air vehicle, but somehow neither he nor Parsons appeared to be injured.

English looked back to his left as he and Parsons took a position on the other side of the jeep. The troop carrier had stopped in the middle of the road and men were scrambling out.

"Grab the machine gun, soldier!"

English replied. "Yes, sir." He then reached into the back of the jeep and grabbed the M16 that he had nonchalantly tossed in there on his COs orders before picking up Parsons.

English and the soldiers positioned at the transport began to return fire. Gunfire continued to roar from the hillside, but it was unclear to English from his position exactly where from.

Assuming the transport had called it in, there would be roughly two minutes until they had air support.

They continued to take heavy fire from up in the hills, but it seemed random to English and he remained uncertain of the origin point. Abruptly it stopped.

Parsons keyed his cell phone. "Woods, check in."

Sergeant Tanya Woods, who had been driving the troop transport quickly responded. "Go ahead, General."

"Report your situation, sergeant."

"We took heavy fire, sir, but we appear to have no casualties other than some cuts and bruises from scrambling out of the vehicle. We have called in air support. ETA 90-seconds."

Parsons looked up at the hillside. He said to no one in particular. "These are either the worst enemy combatants on God's green earth or they were only trying to shake us up."

"Sergeant Woods, when air support arrives …" Parsons head snapped forward and then the General fell into English. English was temporarily blinded.

English realized almost immediately that Parsons was dead, his head had almost literally exploded from what looked to be a very heavy caliber sniper round. He struggled to clear his eyes of Parsons' remains and then felt around for the phone.

Two helicopters crested the hill, search lights blazing.

"The General is down, repeat, the General is down." English could taste blood in his mouth and began to gag as he realized it was not his own.

"How bad?" It was Woods.

"He's fuckin' dead, man. They blew his God damn head off!" More shots rang out, the helicopters began to spin out of control. In moments, they were down. Two fireballs erupted from the hillside about 50-meters from English's jeep.

"Where the fuck are those shots coming from, English!"

English was going into shock. More shots erupted and as English looked to his left, he watched as one by one the soldiers with Sergeant Woods were dropping. Within seconds, they were all down.

English sat against the jeep waiting for the bullet to come. He realized way too late that the snipers were not on the hillside, but rather on the beach. He looked beneath the "Santa Monica Peer" sign that he now realized he was sitting beneath and saw at least three men boarding a small boat. He could not swear to it, but he was fairly certain one waved to him as he boarded.

English heard a chirping sound and realized it had become deathly quiet. No one at the troop transport appeared to be conscious and for all English knew, they were all dead.

The chirping repeated and English looked at Parsons' phone, which was still in his hand. He stared at it for several seconds and then clicked accept.

"General Parsons, please report, sir. We have reports of two choppers down and your squad taking heavy fire."

English continued to stare at the phone. "General, please report."

English felt himself slipping into shock. He could manage, "it was a massacre," before he passed out.

73

May 30, 2026

Washington, District of Columbia

"We stand here today a divided people. This was not my father's vision. He was a uniter and he spent his life and ultimately gave his life in the effort to keep these United States truly united."

President Richard Champer Jr. looked over the large crowd that had been gathered in the National Mall. He smiled to himself of how his father might describe the size of the crowd that stood before him. "The largest ever", he'd say, even though it was not close to true.

"It is with great pride that we dedicate this monument to his great memory. He will now sit eternally in this National Mall, sitting just to the left of one of our other great leaders – Abraham Lincoln – and just to the right of our great monument that stretches to the stars."

The crowd roared with approval as the large tarp was pulled away.

"Dad," Champer turned back to the large statue that had been unveiled. It sat within a large building, purposely designed to be larger than the one that housed the Lincoln and Jefferson memorials. "This will be your final resting place.

May you provide both peace and guidance for those who seek it."

74

July 3rd, 2034

Los Angeles, California

"I need to ask you something."

Karen and Larry sat once again enjoying a glass of wine. Larry noticed that this one was significantly better than the one they had shared the other night. He guessed there was both a celebratory and ominous nature to the wine chosen.

She looked at him. She could feel the wine starting to play funny tricks. "Anything."

He smiled as he realized it was the most intimate thing a woman had said to him in what felt like a lifetime. "What happens after tomorrow?"

She felt a warmth growing from within. "What do you mean?"

Larry shrugged. "I mean, let's say Kennex and I pull this off. Where does it go from there?"

Karen sat staring at him. She had to admit she was a bit disappointed by the question as she found herself hoping that he was going to take this in a different direction. "We have friends who have their own roles to play tomorrow. As I said to you a few days ago, we are the tip of the spear."

Larry took a sip of wine. He had promised himself only one glass as he needed to be sharp tomorrow, but the second one was going down smoother than he liked. "But you can't hope to win, can you?

Karen squinted over her glass of wine. "What do you mean?"

Larry sat back. "This is a train that has moved too far down the track to upend by simply cutting the head off the snake."

Karen gave a sarcastic smile. "You are a walking, talking metaphor, Larry." She paused when he did not respond and then continued. "If you think it's so hopeless, why are you doing this?"

Larry drained his second glass. "Because seeing the Champers lose their grip on power is well worth any price of admission. Beth paid for that with her life and I plan to collect on her debt." He poured himself a little more wine and then continued. "And I'd like to be the first person in history to kill not one, but two presidents."

Karen smiled and then was lost in thought for a moment. "So that's it? Revenge?"

"Isn't that why you are doing this?"

She shrugged. "Maybe, but I have more hope than you do. There are more moving pieces than just what happens at the port tomorrow and I think we can finally start to change the narrative on this terrible world we live in."

Larry stared back for several beats. He didn't need to know or want to know what the other pieces were. He then shifted gears. "Was Santa Monica FOB?"

Karen studied him. "And if it was?" Santa Monica had been portrayed by state run media as an act of terrorism.

"If it was, I think we are at war and sometimes you do things in times of war that are regrettable. Killing General Parsons was a mercy killing, but killing a dozen soldiers who are just doing their jobs is something else."

"Fuck that, Larry. You sign up for this military and you are signing a deal with the devil. You know damn well you are going to be killing civilians no matter how much the powers that be try to couch that in patriotism."

"So it was FOB?"

She nodded and then. "Call it the first real shot fired in the counter-attack."

"I've got to get some sleep."

Karen frowned. "So that's it?"

It was Larry's turn to be unsure of what was meant by the question – was she asking about their argument or something else.

Ten minutes later, Larry lay on the couch in the living room. The room was dark and quiet. The door to Karen's room opened and she stood in the doorway. Light behind her silhouetted her figure. She wore a white tee-shirt that stretched to just above her knees.

"Larry?"

He raised his head. "Yeah?"

"I don't want you to die tomorrow."

Larry smiled in the dark. "I'd like that too."

Karen bit her lip, which Larry was able to make out from his vantage point. "How's the couch?"

"It's fine. I've slept on a lot worse over the years."

She smiled. "I'm sure you have." She paused. "Larry, if I asked you to come in here with me, would you?"

Larry stared at her. "I would." He then paused for several beats. "But Karen?"

She just stared at him. Larry realized in that moment that he had not been this attracted to another human being in a decade.

"Ask me tomorrow night."

Karen continued to stare at him for several more beats and then closed the door.

Larry lay alone again in the dark. He stared at her door and put his head down. This was absolutely crazy he thought to himself. He was almost certain to die the next day and he was flirting with a woman who was almost 20-years his junior. He closed his eyes and started to run through the operation again. After forcing himself to do so several times, he opened his eyes.

Larry kicked out his legs and rose to his feet. He walked to Karen's door and opened it without knocking.

75

July 3rd, 2034

Los Angeles, California

Samuel Murphy's eyes slowly opened. "Water?" He whispered through his dry lips.

The man seated at the side of his bed reached for a Styrofoam cup and put the straw in Murphy's mouth. He then drank down a large gulp.

"Slow down, Detective Murphy."

Murphy's eyes slowly focused and he realized he was talking to Jerry Raymond, who was one of the techs at Central Command. Murphy had used Jerry frequently over the years, primarily to understand something as he was too old to learn the ins and outs of the technology that the police force now used.

Raymond pulled the water away and sat back in his chair.

"I'm assuming you are not here to cheer on my recovery." Murphy's chest throbbed a bit, but other than a couple of cracked ribs, he was no worse the wear for his run-in with John Lawrence.

Raymond opened up a folder he had been holding. "Detective Mason had asked me to look into 212 Reardon before you went over there the other night and I came up with some interesting stuff. I ummm, would have brought it to him, but ..." Raymond's voice trailed off. Mason was still in an induced coma as they waited for the swelling in his throat to go down.

Murphy slowly sat up. "I understand. Tell me what you got. And Jerry, remember who you are telling this too."

Raymond nodded. He had been told by Murphy numerous times over the years to "dumb it down for the dinosaur".

Raymond sat forward and spoke in almost a loud whisper. "Well, as you know all civilians are required to travel with their phones. They can leave them at home, but the moment they go through a checkpoint, they're fried."

Murphy nodded. What a friggin world we live in, he thought to himself for at least the 1,000th time.

"So unless this John Lawrence never goes out or at least never goes through a checkpoint, which is pretty hard to do considering you cannot go outside of a ten block radius without passing through one..."

Murphy interrupted. "Unless the phone he is travelling with is encoded with someone other than John Lawrence."

Raymond smiled. "Precisely – he has two identities."

Murphy frowned. "All due respect, Jerry, but I could have saved you hours of toiling over this file – that part was pretty obvious to me."

Raymond nodded. "I wasn't finished, Detective."

Murphy held out his hand. "Apologies, continue."

"So, we know he is out there travelling with a different phone, so that got me to thinking. Someone is living in the Reardon grid, who doesn't actually belong in the Reardon grid. In other words, someone is passing through one of the checkpoints that you would have to pass through to get back to Reardon, but is not registered as living within the grid. So, if we check every checkpoint for frequent travelers and then crosscheck it with those living in the Reardon grid …"

Murphy interrupted. " … Anyone who doesn't belong is a suspect or maybe even our guy."

Raymond smiled. "Exactly."

"How many checkpoints?"

"Sixteen."

Murphy could feel the anticipation building. "And how many suspects?"

Raymond smiled more broadly. "One."

"Who is it?"

Raymond turned around a photo. "Meet Allen Ripley."

Murphy smiled. "Allen effen Ripley. This guy loves pre-2000's pop culture."

"Who's Allen Ripley?"

Murphy shook his head as he studied the picture. "It was Ellen and forget it." He had not gotten much of a look at Lawrence in the dark and the picture was not jogging any memories. He handed it back to Raymond.

"That the guy?"

Murphy stared out into space for a moment. "Could be, but the room was pitch dark and I didn't really get much of a look. In fact, I didn't get any look at all." Murphy paused as if in thought again and then looked at Raymond. "Jerry, what can we do with this?"

"We've put out a tracer and so far, we are not getting any hits. This is not necessarily surprising as it just means that Ripley has not gone through a checkpoint since we put on the trace."

"What about simply locating where this phone is at the present moment?"

Raymond shook his head. "We can do it, but one of the problems of Champer's rules is that everyone is now required to have their phones on at all times. The towers are bombarded every moment with literally millions of signals, which makes targeting one signal nearly impossible. The best we can do is say that he is in the Reardon grid right now, but we can't even pinpoint the street he is on within the grid."

"Okay, so if he goes out tomorrow, we've got him."

Raymond nodded. "We should have him."

Murphy sat back in his bed. He thought about his conversation with Emma – did he really want to catch this guy? Whoever John Lawrence or Allen Ripley was, he had gone through an awful lot to conceal his identity. He had also been in a position to kill both Murphy and Mason, but had not.

"Jerry, who else knows about this?"

Raymond shrugged. "Just you and I right now."

Murphy nodded. "Okay, let's keep the trace on him for now."

"What about an assault team?"

Murphy shook his head. "I want to track this guy and see what he's up to first. There may be bigger fish to fry at the end of this."

Raymond nodded. "Understood."

Murphy brought his legs around and slowly brought himself to a seated position on the side of the bed.

Raymond rose to help him and Murphy waved him off. "Are you sure this is a good idea?"

Murphy paused to catch his breath. He was sorer than he thought. "I'll be fine. Just need a second."

76

July 4th, 2034

Long Beach, California

Larry stood in line right behind Greg Pierson. Pierson had not yet noticed Larry and Larry was secretly hoping he would not turn around. The guard took Pierson's phone and scanned it. Larry was a bit surprised that Pierson was quiet as he had never known the man to not be going on about something.

As the guard and Pierson waited for the computer to confirm Pierson's clearance, Pierson turned and looked at Larry. A smirk formed on Pierson's face as he stared at Larry. He then gave a small chuckle and shook his head. A moment later the guard said, "you're clear, sir." Pierson nodded at the guard and walked through the checkpoint. He did not acknowledge Larry any further.

Larry handed his phone to the checkpoint guard. The guard scanned the phone and handed it back to Larry. After about ten seconds, the guard nodded to Larry, who gave a slight smile in return.

Larry walked toward the gate. He noticed immediately that there was an extra layer of protection today. Large full body scanners had been set up at the entrance way. Larry was not at all surprised given the guest of honor who would be arriving at 1 PM. FOB had expected extra security and Larry had not brought anything along that would raise any suspicions.

Larry passed through the scanners without raising any alarms and he headed toward Building B, which housed one of several locker rooms. As he walked, he looked over at Kennex's trailer. Kennex stood outside, his hands in his pockets, seemingly observing the men and women as they came in.

77

July 4th, 2034

Long Beach, California

The Nordic Mariner pulled out to sea. Captain Elias Heikkinen stood on the deck and watched the port fade into the distance.

Heikkenen was Finnish by birth; although, he had spent most of his life at sea. He had captained the Mariner for the past four years and had traveled the Pacific sea lanes for the past two.

He usually let his men handle the loading and unloading of freight, but today he had taken a keen interest. While it was unusual for anything to go wrong, Heikkenen wanted to be absolutely sure that the freight was delivered without incident.

His men took note of their captain's unusual excitement about the day's delivery, but not enough to raise any alarm bells. Rather, they were happy to see him in good spirits, as the continued Russian incursions in Eastern Europe had him constantly worried about the family he had left behind more than a decade before.

Freight number 656177741 was lowered into place on the dock. Heikkenen watched as the cranes maneuvered the container. Even though he knew there was little risk of something going wrong, Heikkenen found himself holding his breath.

656177741 would first be moved by forklift to the inspection depot where it would pass through a customs check. If all went according to plan, it would never reach inspection.

78

July 4th, 2034

Los Angeles, California

"We got a hit."

Murphy stood over Raymond's shoulder and looked at the computer screen. "Okay, what do we got?"

Murphy had Jerry Raymond drive him home the night before, surprising Emma, who had assumed he'd be in the hospital for at least another night. He had filled her in on what Raymond had found as she prepared a bath for him.

Emma was initially surprised that Murphy had not assigned an assault team to the case. This would have been SOP and she had been a detective's wife long enough to know it. But before Murphy could explain himself, she realized why he had not – he was unsure of whether he actually wanted to stop John Lawrence or Allen Ripley or whatever his name really was (the two settled on calling him Lawrence).

The two of them discussed the case as Murphy soaked in the bath. He was fairly certain that Jerry Raymond would obey whatever Murphy ordered him to do, but he could not be entirely sure.

Emma had pressed him on what he thought Lawrence was up to and Murphy had to admit that he had absolutely no idea. All he knew was that this guy had tried really hard to hide his identity, apparently for many years and his skills in doing so were the best that Murphy had ever seen.

In the old days, it was relatively easy to live off the grid. But in the new world, with mandatory carry rules for cell phones, cameras watching all the time and checkpoints that were nearly impossible to avoid (not to mention cops and army everywhere), living off the grid was nearly impossible.

Murphy had gotten to the office early and had dutifully sat through the morning briefing. Because it was parade day and the President was in town, the briefing, which typically ran about twenty minutes, stretched to nearly an hour. Murphy, who was still a bit groggy from the events of the past few days, struggled not to zone out. The moment the briefing was over, Murphy made his way to Raymond's desk.

Jerry Raymond looked back over his shoulder at Murphy. He said in the same loud whisper he had used in the hospital, "Ripley passed through three checkpoints this morning." Raymond pointed at the screen. "Here, which is him leaving the Reardon grid, here and here. I pulled the logs on all three and he's been passing through these three pretty regularly over the past few years."

Murphy pulled over a chair that was behind Raymond's desk and sat next to him. "So he missed the July fourth parade?"

Raymond nodded. "It would appear so. He is obviously heading away from the parade route."

Murphy stared at the screen. He realized that he had reached a delicate spot. Had Murphy followed standard procedure, they would almost certainly have Lawrence/Ripley in custody as they would have easily been able to grab him at one of the checkpoints.

At the very least, they had him for the attempted murder of two police officers, which carried the death penalty. Jerry Raymond had not brought this up and he seemed to be going along with Murphy, but Murphy was not sure how long this would last.

"What's your best guess on where he was heading?"

Raymond studied the map on his screen. After about ten seconds, he responded. "This last one here leads to a few places, but I'd say he either ends up at the port or at the armory."

"Don't they have checkpoints at both?"

Raymond nodded. "They do, but they are not connected to the grid. Only the primary checkpoints get uploaded, while those checkpoints used to protect businesses are just a traditional ID check."

Murphy sat back in his chair and considered what they had. At the very least, he had to order an assault team pick-up of Lawrence/Ripley when he passed back through the checkpoints later in the day. The question was whether he needed to or wanted to do anything before that.

"Okay, Jerry. This is great work by you. I am going to order assault teams at these checkpoints, so we get him picked up. I am also going to put your name forward for a commendation."

Raymond smiled. "Thanks, Detective. Just doing the job."

About five minutes later, Murphy sat in his office. He called up the morning briefing on his computer. He then clicked to the President's schedule.

When Jerry had said the port was a likely destination for Lawrence/Ripley, a light had gone on for Murphy. He had been zoned out in much of the morning briefing, but one could not help but pay attention when the briefing discussed the President's itinerary.

Murphy stared at the computer screen. Was Lawrence/Ripley going to cross paths with the President today? Was there some kind of plot here or was this just a wild coincidence?

Murphy's gut and 25-years of experience told him there were no coincidences that went this far.

Murphy clicked off his computer and rose to his feet. He was still moving gingerly and probably would for several more days. He grabbed his blazer, which was hung on the back of his chair and put it on. He then clicked a button on his cellphone.

"Depot, go ahead."

"This is Detective Murphy, I am going to need a vehicle."

79

July 4th, 2034

Long Beach, California

Jack Kennex watched Larry through his office window. He seemed to be going about his work with his normal gusto and Kennex saw no obvious alarm bells in which to call off the mission.

The large stack of freight from which Larry had been working was slowly getting whittled down. Kennex stared at the pile momentarily and then forced himself to get back to his paperwork.

He looked at the iPad sitting on his desk and he momentarily ran his fingers over it. He could feel a twinge of nerves building in his belly.

80

July 4th, 2034

Los Angeles, California

The motorcade rumbled down the 110 freeway. The secret service had done a quick walk through the port the day before, but this was logistically a difficult exercise for them as they had both the parade to worry about and a variety of high-profile public appearances throughout the day.

"ETA sixteen minutes."

The agents reflexively checked their fire-arms. The lone female agent on Champer's team took a deep breath and stared out the window of the SUV that ran just ahead of Champer's.

As she holstered her weapon, she thought to herself, "mom, dad, today is for you,"

81

July 4th, 2034

Long Beach, California

Larry stepped off of the forklift and moved to the front. He bent down to check one of the blades, which he then began to fiddle with.

Workers were scrambling around as the motorcade would be arriving in about fifteen minutes and they had all been ordered to stand in lines when it was ten minutes out.

Most of the President's advance team was stationed by the gates and by the shoreline in order to keep any unwanteds out of the port, which made moving around inside the gates a bit easier than Larry had feared it would be.

Larry shook the blade up and down and did a quick scan to see if anyone had focused on what he was doing. Everyone seemed preoccupied with finishing up their various tasks.

Larry stood up and instead of walking back the short way to his seat on the forklift, he took the long way. Anyone who had been watching would have seen him disappear at the side of one of the large containers of freight.

Larry looked at the label on the container –
656177741.

Larry pressed a button on the left side and a small
door slid up revealing a keypad. He quickly typed
seven numbers into the keypad. As he hit the sixth
number, he paused and looked at his watch. He
then pressed the seventh number as his watch hit
precisely 12:55. A loud horn sounded as he pressed
the pound sign. The door to 656177741 buzzed and
rose at the same moment the horn went off.

Larry reflexively looked into the black void of the
open container and then walked back to the
forklift. Anyone passing the freight would see that
it was open, but Larry was banking that no one
would in the few minutes until the President
arrived.

Larry deftly shifted the forklift into reverse and
turned it around. The other workers had begun to
line-up, so Larry put the lift into top gear and drove
it across the platform. He decided to leave it just
inside the parking depot and he ran quickly to his
spot in the long line as soldiers began to yell at any
stragglers.

82

July 4th, 2034

Long Beach, California

The gates to the port opened as the motorcade approached. The checkpoint guards stood saluting; although, their weapons had been left in the armory as they were not allowed to be armed in the presence of the President.

The motorcade, which consisted of two army troop carriers, two army jeeps with Browning M2 mounted machine guns affixed to turrets in their back seats and six black Lincoln Navigator SUVs, did not slow at the gates, but instead pulled inside the gates of the port and stopped in one long row.

The dockworkers stood in two long lines that were three deep on each side of the motorcade. The only movement from the motorcade came from the jeeps as the mounted M2's slowly tracked back and forth across the line of workers.

Soldiers then began to spill out of the two troop carriers that were stationed at the front and back of the motorcade. They took positions on either end and essentially created a human shield should anyone decide that they wanted to attack from either the east or the west. To the north and south, large stacks of freight provided a natural defense against anyone who thought to attack the President.

83

July 4th, 2034

Long Beach, California

Jack Kennex hunched his shoulders and bent his neck a little lower. He had tried out the space under his desk the week before and he knew he could fit with his back against one side and his feet touching the other. He had imagined himself as a sort of human accordion and while it wasn't comfortable to squeeze his 240 pound frame under his desk, it worked for what he needed to do.

Kennex placed the iPad on his knees and looked at the screen. He clicked on the program, which quickly loaded. The clock on the iPad said 1:03. The itinerary called for the President to exit his vehicle at 1:05.

They had decided last night that they would go precisely at 1:08. The President's itinerary was chock full of events on the day and his detail would likely want to keep him on schedule.

Kennex ran through the controls in his mind one more time. He figured he would have two or three passes and he could not afford to screw any of them up.

He activated the viewer on the program and he realized that he was now seeing through the eyes of the program. He focused the lens and waited.

84

July 4th, 2034

Long Beach, California

Detective Murphy stood at the far end of one of the line of workers. He looked out across the platform to the ocean, which was about 300 meters from where he stood. He could see a small sliver of water as most of it was obstructed by the towers of freight that were piled along the dock. He could not see any ships from where he stood and he assumed that most had been ordered out of port because of the President's arrival.

As he stood there, Murphy was unsure of what he was looking for. He had an image of Allen Ripley, but there were several hundred men on the dock and it was like looking for a needle in a haystack. He also was not sure he actually wanted to find Ripley.

And then he did. Standing in the opposite line in the front row, his face was unmistakable to Murphy.

Murphy reflexively patted his left breast and was reminded that he had checked his firearm at the armory when he arrived.

Ripley appeared to be focused on the President's motorcade, which was not particularly unusual as most at the port were looking in the same direction.

The doors to the SUVs began opening and several secret service agents began fanning out in front of the crowd. Murphy noted to himself that one of them was a woman. He did a double take when he looked at her, not because he recognized her, but because he was surprised that she appeared to be Latino.

A moment later, the doors to the President's SUV opened and President Richard Champer Jr. stepped out and waved to the crowd.

Six secret service agents flanked the President as he moved to the far end of the line to begin shaking hands.

85

July 4ᵗʰ, 2034

Long Beach, California

1:07:35. Kennex took a deep breath. He had to assume Nash had done his job or else there was going to be a terrible racket.

Dougherty had trained him the week before on the software, but it had only been a simulation as there was no safe place to do a test run. They had also not thought to do it with Kennex 'pretzled' underneath a desk, which added another challenge.

1:07:55. Kennex rubbed his palms against the sides of his legs to dry them.

At precisely 1:08:00, he pressed the ignition button and the image on his screen immediately began to shake.

86

July 4th, 2034

Long Beach, California

Murphy heard the sound before anyone else as he stood closest to the large freight container. He watched Champer step from the SUV and led by six secret service agents, he made his way toward the line of dockworkers opposite Murphy.

To Murphy's right and toward the ocean, a sound which resembled an engine powering up began to emanate from somewhere within the pile of freight.

Murphy looked for where the sound was coming from, but he could not locate it in the large stack. He then turned back to the President and his detail. No one seemed to notice the engine noise.

He then looked at Ripley, who also appeared to take no notice of the noise. In fact, as he looked at the crowd, no one, save for one man appeared to be looking at the freight pile – they were all transfixed by the presence of Champer.

Champer and his men were approaching Ripley. Champer reached into the crowd, shaking the odd hand. He passed Ripley, who happily shook Champer's hand with a big smile.

The entourage then moved on. If it were Ripley's plan to attack the President directly, his best opportunity had just passed.

87

July 4th, 2034

Long Beach, California

The female secret service agent was the first one to look up as the drone roared from the open freight container. The other agents and the soldiers who had positioned themselves at the ends of the motorcade were momentarily confused.

The drone banked overhead just above the shoreline and then began an approach toward the President's motorcade and the mass of dockworkers.

Most in the mass of men and women had now noticed the strange aerial vehicle that was roughly the size of a large glider fast approaching their position. However, no one made any effort to move, but rather stood there transfixed by the approaching plane.

A rocket streaked from the large black drone hitting the army jeep positioned at the front of the motorcade head on. It exploded instantly in a massive fireball.

A second rocket streaked toward the President's entourage, but overshot them by ten feet. The rocket clipped the mass of men lined up to greet the President, killing ten instantly and wounding countless others.

All hell had broken loose.

88

July 4th, 2034

Long Beach, California

Champer felt his head get pushed down as the second rocket streaked overhead.

He did not see, but could hear the explosion and the screams that followed.

"Go, go, go," he heard one of his detail yell and then he heard gunfire all around him. He forced his head up as the agents pushed him toward the SUV closest to them. He saw several agents pointing their guns to the sky and firing wantonly. He was still not sure what was happening.

The heat from the fires was intense and Champer could literally feel his skin beginning to burn as the agents pushed him closer to the burning jeep and one of the SUVs.

A moment later, the agent in front of him fell to the ground. Champer stumbled over his body. He fell to one knee and felt hands grab him under his arms to quickly lift him back to his feet. He then saw that the agent he had just stumbled over had been shot in the head. Champer was briefly reminded of his father lying in state on board Air Force 1.

And then the SUV they were pushing him toward exploded in a massive fireball.

89

July 4th, 2034

Long Beach, California

Naomi Hamilton, who had been born Naomi Lopez 31-years ago, thought about her parents as she drew her Glock. The drone pilot had missed on what was likely to be his best shot at Champer.

The remaining army jeep had pointed its M2 machine gun toward the sky, while soldiers armed with machine guns were attempting to pick off the drone as it circled overhead. The drone was banking over the entry gate and looking to prepare to make another approach.

Her parents were good people. They had literally committed one criminal act in their lives — illegally crossing the Mexico/US border. Besides that, they had lived the lives of honest, upstanding people, who never hesitated to help those in need whenever they could.

They had been rewarded with deportation and a bullet to the back of the head.

Naomi pointed her gun at Gus Taylor and shot him in the head. Gus was a good man, but he was in front of the President and the President was going to die today. Naomi fired again, this time at the President, but at the moment she pulled the trigger, she was hit hard from behind by the concussion of another explosion. She was thrown to the ground, her back screaming in pain and the wind knocked from her lungs.

As she lay there, Naomi thought of her sisters and of her parents. Her right hand pawed the ground for the gun that now lay somewhere in the mayhem.

90

July 4th, 2034

Long Beach, California

Murphy stood frozen as the events unfolded around him. Men were running in every direction and soldiers and secret service agents were firing randomly at the drone flying overhead.

Murphy watched as the female secret service agent shot another agent and then was blown to the ground by an exploding vehicle. He doubted the woman had meant to do it, but he could not figure out in the moment what she had been aiming at.

Two Blackhawk helicopters streaked in from the north. At the same moment, Murphy watched another man pick up the female agent's gun. Murphy didn't recognize the man, but something about the way he moved reminded him of something.

Murphy then saw Ripley running toward a trailer and that was finally enough to snap the detective out of his fugue-like state. Murphy ran diagonally toward the trailer in an effort to cut Ripley off. Ripley appeared to be running with a limp, which again struck Murphy as odd given how he had gotten the jump on Mason and Murphy. At that moment, Murphy realized he was unarmed and would be challenging Ripley with only his fists.

91

July 4th, 2034

Long Beach, California

Nash picked up the female agent's gun. He had watched her try to shoot the President, but the drone rocket had thrown off her aim. Nash thought of his own misfortune with aim and how that had been in large part responsible for the next decade of his life.

Nash looked up as two rockets from the incoming helicopters flew overhead. Both missed the drone, which was now making its third approach, and flew to the west. Larry assumed they had impacted the ocean as he could not make out the sound of any explosion.

Larry checked the female agent for a pulse. It was faint, but she was alive. He realized at that moment that there was nothing he could do to help her and she might be better off dying on the platform.

Larry leveled the Glock and looked for the President. Out of the corner of his field of vision he caught a small circle of secret service agents pushing the President toward one of the three remaining SUVs.

The drone fired two more rockets. As they streaked in, the drone awkwardly veered left and Larry realized that it had been hit.

Larry focused back on the President. His men had pivoted away from the SUVs and toward Kennex's trailer as the incoming rockets slammed into the remaining line-up of vehicles.

Larry rose to his feet and began running after Champer and the group of agents. As he ran, he heard what he assumed was the drone crashing into a large stack of freight somewhere to his left.

92

July 4th, 2034

Long Beach, California

Murphy arrived at the steps of the trailer at nearly the same moment as Ripley. He slammed into his left side and Murphy was surprised how easily he took the man to the ground.

Ripley grunted under Murphy's weight. He then said between winded gasps, "please man, get off me!"

Murphy pushed his knee into Ripley's back. He had neither handcuffs, nor a gun, so all he could think to do was hold Ripley there and wait for help.

Murphy looked up as a group of secret service agents bared down on his location. A moment later, the two agents in front raised their handguns. Murphy reflexively raised his hands in surrender. The agents barreled past Murphy and Ripley, pushing the President into the trailer that sat to Murphy's left

As they entered the trailer, several bullets smacked the door of the trailer and the mass of men that was pushing inside. One agent fell just outside the door. He appeared to have been shot in the back of the head.

The dead agent's gun lay just behind Murphy and without getting off of Ripley, he reached back and scrambled to pick it up.

Murphy grabbed the gun and turned as a foot connected with his chest. He fell backward winded from the blow.

93

July 4th, 2034

Long Beach, California

Nash ran with the Glock raised. He fired five times at the mass of men as they reached the door to Kennex's trailer. He was not sure if he had hit the President, but he did hit at least two of the agents.

He saw the man, who was sitting atop another man, reaching for a weapon. Nash kept his stride and kicked out his left foot as the man turned, catching him flush in the chest. Larry was not sure how many bullets he had left and he didn't want to waste one.

Larry stopped at the door to the trailer. He realized in that moment he was probably about to die as the agent's would shoot anyone who came through the door. He grabbed the handle and took two deep breaths.

94

July 4th, 2034

Long Beach, California

Kennex rose to his feet. One of the agent's pressed a gun against the back of his head.

"What the fuck are you doing in here?"

"I'm just hiding, man. It's fucking crazy out there."

Kennex looked down at the broken iPad. When he had lost the drone's signal, Kennex had smashed the device against the corner of the desk.

Kennex then focused in on the President. He realized at that moment that he had failed.

The door to the trailer flew open. The agents raised their guns.

95

July 4th, 2034

Long Beach, California

Champer's right side ached and his ears were ringing, but he otherwise felt like he had survived the worst of it.

The agents were frantically trying to raise help, while the dockworker, who had been hiding in the trailer, stood behind his desk with his arms raised.

The door flew open. At the same moment, the dockworker dove over the desk, causing the agent behind him to fire. Inside the closed quarters of the trailer, the gunshot sounded like a stick of dynamite going off.

The agents momentarily turned their heads away from the door as the gun exploded. A man stood in the doorway and fired five times. He then stepped into the trailer and closed the door.

Champer pushed himself up against the wall. All around him, the secret service agents appeared to be dead or dying.

The dockworker who had been under the desk was lying face-down on the floor. A large blood stain was forming in the middle of his back and blood was streaming from his mouth.

Champer looked up at the man who had just dispatched of his entire secret service detail.

96

July 4th, 2034

Long Beach, California

Nash looked down at Jack Kennex's body. He had been shot in the back and Larry could tell by the blood stain on his shirt and the blood coming from his mouth that Kennex was dead.

Larry raised the gun and pointed it at Champer, who stood cowering against the wall. Larry pulled the trigger, but the gun simply clicked. He was out of bullets.

Larry stepped forward and punched Champer in the jaw. He fell to the ground at Larry's feet.

Through broken teeth and a broken nose, Champer said, "please, don't."

Larry picked up one of the agent's guns and locked eyes with Champer.

97

July 4th, 2034

Long Beach, California

"Please, don't." Champer could taste blood, which was flowing from his nose and mouth.

Champer locked eyes with the man standing above him. He stared at the gun and then back at those deep blue eyes. As the gun exploded, Champer had a moment of recognition.

July 4th, 2034

Long Beach, California

Larry came up for air. His right side burned badly and he could tell that he was losing a fair bit of blood. He scanned the port and could not see anyone in pursuit. He then dove again and continued to swim along the shoreline away from the port. The current was strong, but even wounded, Larry had always been a powerful swimmer and he was able to remain about 50-meters from shore, swimming due north.

The last five minutes had been a whirlwind.

He had shot Champer twice in the head. He was pretty sure at the final moment that Champer had recognized him, which gave Larry some satisfaction. Jack Kennex along with countless other innocent people had died today, but at least the Champer dynasty was at an end.

Larry had quickly exited the trailer and come face to face with the man who he had kicked before entering the trailer. Another man lay on the ground next to him. The standing man pointed a gun at Larry and for a moment Larry had been certain he was going to fire.

"Did you get him?"

Larry stood there in shock for a moment and then gave the man a slight nod. Larry realized the man who was lying on the ground was Greg Pierson, who Larry had 'tagged' with the Allen Ripley identity as another means of evasion.

"You'll need to kill him." Larry pointed at Pierson.

The man looked down at Pierson. He looked back at Larry, who again gave a slight nod. As Pierson cried out, "no wait," the man fired one shot into the back of Pierson's head.

Larry stared at the man for another beat and then the man waved his gun to the right. "Go."

Larry nodded again and then started running. All around him, chaos reigned.

At least seven vehicles were on fire, while to Nash's right, a huge stack of freight was burning and had partially collapsed on itself. As he ran, Larry guessed that this was where the drone had met its ultimate demise.

Soldiers ran this way and that, machine guns raised. No one seemed to have theater authority and thus no one was as of yet being arrested or at least held in custody, which was the logical thing to do at this point, since the immediate threat seemed to be over.

Larry heard screams from behind him, they had apparently found the carnage in the trailer.

Larry reached a line of cargo and cut between the large boxes. Above him, several helicopters circled and then Larry heard gunfire.

Someone yelled "stop" and Larry dug in and ran even harder. Just as he was about to turn the corner around the large stack of freight, a bullet bit into his right side. Larry momentarily stumbled but then he was around the corner and out of the line of fire.

His side burned badly, but even in a dead run, he could tell it was not immediately fatal. The cold seawater would help to stem the bleeding – he just needed to make it there.

Larry wasn't sure if there would be any soldiers left along the shoreline. He suspected or rather hoped that the mayhem that had just taken place inland would have drawn them all away from the shore in an effort to protect the President. If any of them had stayed behind, Larry was unlikely to make it past them in his current state.

Larry could now see the edge of the water. He ran past four wounded dockworkers, who had apparently stumbled down to the waterfront in hopes of escaping the carnage. They watched as

Larry hit the edge of the shoreline and dove 20-feet down into the Pacific waters.

As he hit the water, his side screamed out in pain and Larry was temporarily winded. As he propelled his arms forward, he was pleased to learn that he still had a reasonable range of motion despite the gunshot wound.

He pushed out with his arms and legs and fought against the current in an effort to get away from shore. After about forty seconds of hard swimming, he surfaced to catch his breath and do a quick assessment.

No one stood on the docks pointing at him or pointing guns at him and the helicopters overhead seemed preoccupied with the events onshore. Larry again dove beneath the surface and continue to push his way north up the coast.

He figured he had about thirty minutes to get clear and out of the water. Beyond that, the wound in his back may prove more problematic, while someone was likely to remember a crazy redhead diving into the ocean.

99

July 4th, 2034

Long Beach, California

Naomi Hamilton heard the screams, which were coming to the north of her. "The President is down!"

The heat from the fires, which were about twenty feet from her position, was intense. Her back screamed in pain and she assumed that she had significant shrapnel lodged in her back and legs.

She could feel her consciousness beginning to fade and she struggled to focus her hearing as several soldiers had wandered near her position and were discussing the mayhem that had taken place. No one made any effort to provide her with medical assistance as there were bigger fish to fry this day.

As the last wisps of consciousness faded, Naomi was sure she heard the words "shot twice in the head".

She died smiling.

100

July 4th, 2034

Los Angeles, California

Karen sat at the kitchen table and stared at the television screen. Her satellite phone had rang almost an hour before to report explosions at the port, but since then, nothing. Fox News, which was the only network licensed to report in the OZ had yet to report on anything out of the ordinary.

Ken Dougherty walked into the kitchen and sat down at the table across from Karen. "Humphries called. The eastern grid operation was a success."

Karen gave a slight smile, but this did not hide the nervous look on her face. "Any reports from New York?"

Dougherty shook his head. "Not yet."

They both sat in silence for several seconds and then abruptly turned to the television as the distinctive sound of "Fox Breaking News" cut into the newscast.

"Fox breaking news, I'm Simone Simon in New York. Reports coming in from the California Occupied Zone of a terrorist attack at the Long Beach port. We go to Kelly Carter, who is near the scene."

Dougherty looked at Karen. "Here we go."

"Thanks, Simone. I am currently standing about half a mile from the port, which is as close as we can get at this time. As you can see behind me, there are a number of Apache helicopters flying overhead and the situation remains active."

"Information is still spotty, but apparently there has been an attack at the port involving unknown aircraft and potentially the use of chemical agents. We do not have as of yet and word on casualties or whether or not the terrorists, who have brazenly attacked our country, are in custody."

"Thanks, Kelly. Any word on the President? He was in California today for the parade and I know a lot of folks will be worried about him."

Carter paused as there was a slight delay to the feed from the Fox studios in New York. She then shook her head. "Nothing yet, Simone. As I said, information has been spotty up until now."

Karen looked at Dougherty. "They got him."

"How can you be sure?"

"Because if he was alive, Fox would make sure we all knew it and they'd spin it in such a way that he heroically saved the day. I'm telling you, Ken. Jack and Nash did it."

A moment later, Karen's phone buzzed.

"Karen, it's Dutch."

Karen stood up and looked at Dougherty as she held the phone to her ear. "Dutch, how are you?"

Dougherty rose as well and started pacing around the room.

"A little tired. I hurt my back pretty badly. But we finished the job."

She looked at Dougherty and frowned. "And did you have a chance to see James?"

There was a pause. "I'm sorry but James won't be coming."

Karen was silent for a moment. "I understand."

"And I won't be coming either."

Karen began to cry. "Dutch, I don't think that's a good idea. We have lots of friends here who would love to see you and help you with your back."

"You and I both know that's not a good idea."

"I don't care. You come and see us!"

"I have to go."

"Dutch, don't go."

"I have to go."

"Larry, please, don't!"

The line went dead. Karen looked at Dougherty.

"Jack?"

She looked at him and shook her head.

End Book One

Made in the USA
Middletown, DE
02 February 2022

60298384R00239